The May Queen

Helen Irene Young

CROOKED
CAT

First Red Line Edition
Crooked Cat Publishing Ltd. 2017

Discover us online:
www.crookedcatbooks.com

Join us on facebook:
www.facebook.com/crookedcatbooks

*Tweet a photo of yourself holding
this book to **@crookedcatbooks**
and something nice will happen.*

#mayqueenbook

Praise for The May Queen:

'An unsettling coming-of-age tale.'
Good Housekeeping

'A beautifully written first novel.'
Cotswold Life

'Edible prose, waspish humour and a lot of heart.'
Jonathan Eyers,
author of The Thieves of Pudding Lane

'Lively writing and skilfully portrayed family
dynamics.'
Emma Dally,
author of Remembered Dreams

'A bright and daring heroine.'
Read 50

For Frances

Acknowledgements

Thank you Antonia, Fiona, Jess and Joe. Cheers Karen, Laura, Maggie and Mia. You too Phil, Roger, Rohan and Rose. Life will never be the same again, Richard.

Dad, you encouraged me first and David, you after. Gerald, we made it.

Carolina, Clare and Jo, thanks for distracting. Laura, my creative better.

Lastly, Laurence, Miriam and Steph at Crooked Cat. Miaow

About the Author

Helen is a digital editor. In a former life, she worked as a bookseller for Waterstones and an admissions assistant for an acting school, before signing up to a £12-a-day internship at a glossy magazine (when it was the norm). For the next six years (and on a better grade) she went on to write and edit for Harper's Bazaar and Good Housekeeping. She is currently the website editor for Bloomsbury Publishing.

Helen attended the Faber Novel Writing Programme. She splits her time between London, Wiltshire and Colombia, when she can get there. The May Queen is her debut novel.

@helenireneyoung

The May Queen

PART ONE

1934
JULY

It was the first thing to come between May and the carnival. That crack, wallop of flesh against flesh, crying out into the night like two beasts in the barn. Only it wasn't two in the dirt, like the boys dared her look at, but Ma and Sophie in the kitchen, thrashing out in other ways.

"Who did it? Tell me, girl, and tell me now." Ma's question came sounding like a threat.

Inside the room, Sophie stayed silent, one hand raised to the spreading sting.

Outside, May knew there was safety in keeping shut when Ma got up in one of her fits – cast often when the sisters came home past curfew or had been out robbing eggs – precious small blues and greens. "They're nature's, not yours," Ma would say, tossing them into the garden so they fell open and feast-like for the coots.

May drank up the scene in front like one looking on at a picture – through the solid square lens of the window.

"Wait till Pa hears."

"Ma, you wouldn't!"

"He'll know soon enough without me telling; look at you."

May took the invitation not given and looked, her mouth opening to form the soft O that Sophie's hands went down around like a ripe apple. Where'd she been to get that, May puzzled, calling up the hours spent planning costumes day after day. Costumes not needed for a year but deliberately mapped, in case just maybe, first prize favoured the long-travelled approach.

May shivered, her cotton dress caught between dry and

not. She leant against the wall in front, finding comfort in its heat. The day had blistered to make the stone glow now, long after the light had left it. A day most spent dripping in their skin, while May writhed cool through the currents of the mill pond. Out of sight, just.

"What have I done?" Ma asked of the low ceiling, raising both arms up high but finding no answer there.

Sophie didn't look up, seeming returned to saying nothing, except now she whimpered. Whimpered like that otter May had come upon the year previous beneath the bridge. It was hiding when she crept close, a finger raised to closed lips to say she wouldn't tell. It had a wide tear in its side where a film of liquid puddled. Crouching nearby, she waited, while downstream, past the back of The Bull and a distance gone, the water bailiffs worked on with their otterhounds, sniffing out new fur. Then she was alone again, listening to the water babble and the hounds call off they'd found another. "No matter how deep you dive, they'll find you," Sophie had whispered, so serious that May never slept a wink the whole time of year they came looking.

"You've done it, the shame you have," brought Ma's fists down punching on the wood table that divided her from Sophie.

"Ma!"

"You ain't no girl of mine."

"Who knows, hey? Who, who?" came sounding new from Ma, who given up on the table and the ceiling before, sent echoing over to the big white sink. Sophie looked like she waited for some answer back and May, outside, did too but only a menace, pest fox call tightened her shoulder tops. It was far off in a field and she didn't turn, but took to gripping at the window ledge, playing with the shadow that found half her fingers, pushing the tips to glow like they had crept into the room and she had not.

What about when Pa returns? May thought.

"When Pa's home you'll get it," spoke Ma now, like she'd reached inside May's head for that one, sensing her youngest child close, drawing reserves like some great trunk from a sapling.

"I'll leave," shrieked Sophie and it was the most solid thing she'd done, seeming like trickled water till then, that both May and Ma stepped back and looked to see if she'd repeat the cry or go back to babbling.

"Yes, I reckon you shall," came Ma more quiet, moving round the plank. "And if you won't tell me his name, I'll get it from one does know," she said still going, right past like she'd missed her target: "May! No use hiding if you can't keep hidden." Ma pulled her through the open door and into the room.

"She don't know, so don't ask her," said Sophie, seeking out May's sewn-shut lips.

"You're wet through, girl," brought Ma's hand down semi-circular to come stinging against her calves.

May wrestled free and stood backed into a corner, like she didn't take to being infected with either of their nonsense.

"What I say about swimming in that pond?"

"Not to."

"You ain't no girl now you've got woman's ways. You want to end like her?" A shaky finger lined up Sophie in its sights.

May thought on how the answer weren't the one Ma wanted.

"Do you?" grabbed Ma at her sleeves, wringing her out like washday suds.

Next thing she knew, Sophie lay on the floor at both their feet, where she'd come running and met Ma's anger at the end of the line.

AUGUST

May lay in the garden beneath the sheets, not yet fixed on whether to watch them come dry completely. Every time the wind ploughed through the line of milky white, the sun flashed bright across her face. She yawned like a cat and stretched out, uncurling tightened limbs, tanned by days beneath the scorch. A strip of golden skin ran round her neck, exposing the flesh there like precious metal. When Ma went into the village, it was possible still to slip into the mill pond and find relief. Anchoring her feet between the cold crevices on the slimy bottom, she kept her mouth below, because she liked the tingly coolness of the water there.

"May, you come in and help finish what you started," Ma called, standing in the frame.

May rolled onto her stomach and pushed up off the grass. Inside, the chaos of washday slopped in puddles on the floor.

"You push the mangle back, and mind that bucket, girl," Ma said.

May watched the liquid dance at her feet before searching up high for the water jug.

"Oh, get comfortable, why don't you?" said Ma as May poured and then drank beneath her dried-out stare.

"Where's this go?" May asked, lifting the leaky bucket.

"If I've said once, I've said thousand times, outside in the pond."

But the ducks don't want it, May thought, remaining there. Ma went to leave off clattering at the fireside to direct her better, but May made sharp her exit. She opened the side gate and swung bucket-in-hand towards the still surface of the mill pond. Water submerged the sluice gate, connecting the bricks below the surface with the outlying pool. The gate was clotted stiff by centuries of algae, shipwreck-like. She knew better than them in the village to go diving there for buried treasure, keeping secret what Pa had given years back, a pirate's knife rusted down like an old nail. So she had no need to make a further friend of curiosity, he'd said.

It was here she poured the pail, the sweat from their lives falling muddy between the gratings, not spread slick-like over the moorhen nests and bullfinches as before. That's one thing done different now it's me, she thought somewhat guiltily. She'd often seen Sophie visit the same spot months back, labouring over another sort of liquid, washed quickly from sight by a bucket full of fresh from the pond. Ma must have guessed it weren't her cooking done it.

She looked up. There weren't many out, not on the road across the bridge with its steady iron railings, linking Fairford to the world beyond their grasp. But it was still early, maybe tipping at midday if the sun said right.

Like most times, May's thoughts turned to the other river, upstream beyond the wall. There, it was called the Serpentine and curved through the landscape like stretched toffee. Big House claimed it, and it was off limits to all folk but them and Pa and Pa's lot who worked there. There weren't nothing to look at, even standing on the upturned bucket. May could see more from her bedroom window. On moonlit nights, it was clearer still, and she'd open her eyes wide so their pools would drink deep, feeding her dreams with firefly flickers of a life she weren't likely to touch this year, next, or the ones to creep in after.

When she got back to the kitchen, Ma had already stowed away the last of the cast-iron tubs and brought down the flames, so the water in the pot, like an old man's belly, simmered less angrily. Right now, Ma was caught busy twisting unused line around her arm and it was all May could do to move aside before being hit by a bundle.

"To be worked on, that one," said Ma.

May picked it up and the two wound in silence, the younger watching how the elder held it taut on the journey between elbow and palm.

"When she coming back?" May asked.

"Didn't say, last she wrote."

"She wrote?"

"Course, think I don't know what my own daughter's doing?"

May let the rope go slack.

"Easy girl, making more work for yourself that way of thinking."

"I weren't thinking much."

"You was enough; now concentrate, Pa needs his lunch."

"Think you might let me take it?"

"I might," Ma said, resting down the neat ball like a newly formed planet. "Got to be firm, May, otherwise it gets the better of you," she said, going over and correcting the sagging loops.

Like washday, going up to see Pa fell to Sophie's lot. Sophie had the trust of it, like being older made her less a child. She, grown ahead, always had the best from Ma's endless list of doings, May scratched over, with small mean thoughts she shouldn't have owned – "growth stunters", Ma called them. Then Sophie was gone and in the dust cloud that followed, choking Ma late at night when her shadow sat quiet, May came through with stature. Since then she courted duty, like one raised up, honeymoon-new.

It was with this encouragement, May left Ma torturing slices from the ham and, kicking off her gumboots, flung upstairs for better shoes. There she found brown lace-ups with something like a shine to them after spit.

She bounded down and had to be held firm whilst Ma put instructions into her head for how to behave beyond the wall where the Serpentine waited. For one long-practised underwater, the thought of it made her eyes sting. May cocked her head to hope at hearing it hiss and stretch, but instead, caught Ma's drowning clatter.

"Them folk don't want you running around a pest and falling in," Ma said, cooling May's cheeks with the rough side of a damp cloth, all the time making her fears talk. May bore it; being licked clean by Ma's rough words, wondering what became of that pirate's knife. If true danger waited on the serpent side, Sophie didn't tell of it. Besides, at the snake's mouth was Big House, and she'd been there on carnival days before. There'd been a crowd, though. Ma let go and a cloth bag of perishables followed soon after.

"Any message, then?" May turned on the threshold, swinging Pa's lunch to test the weight of it.

"I'm not sure," Ma said, squinting like the wind had changed, before the answer rumbled true: "Potatoes. Bring back a prize couple if he can."

The kitchen gardens were nestled at the back of Big House. But where nestling implied cosiness – a tiny bird snug in a roost – they were not. A vast complex of glass and wrought iron spread across the landscape. Lines of lean stalks propped up the bean house, while in the root veg hall, dusty beds squatted low. Beside these, weird fruits and plants vied for space in the hot houses. Athletic leaves and stems pumped full of water spread their mass far and wide, brash in comparison to the genteel roses braving the native soil outside. In the open, the formal gardens gave way to vegetable plots and then fields, which stretched so far into the distance, May long ago concluded that Big House didn't know where it ended and the rest of the world began.

May released the catch on the back gate and swung out past the mill pond towards the door to the park. She passed the pond; the water was quiet today, the ducks and swans splashing about downstream beyond the bridge. She fought the thumping need to dive, shoes and all. May got to the gate and pushed on into the park. It banged shut heavy behind. On this side, everything seemed slowed. The land had that sleepy feeling found after cocoa. The grass along the bank was clipped short – even the ducks had a certain elegance, dancing across the surface of the water, where the ones near the mill only flapped and shrilled. May slowed right down, too. The Serpentine widened when she turned a bend in the path and she caught her breath at the beauty of it, seeing willows lining the bank, dipping their leaves in its coolness. She passed opposite a miniature pavilion on the far bank, as good a house she'd ever seen. The crafts inside bobbed against their berths as though trying to get somewhere. Their movement reminded May to do the same, and she picked up her pace.

Big House came into view. It startled May how different it looked to the uninvited, as she was then, blinking at her glazed through a hundred eyes. She kept hers upon it as she crossed the stone bridge, the last outpost between her world and that ahead. This was the route Pa took, and the others who lived in the mill buildings. May cast a last look down river to home, unable to believe the mill existed at all from here. Even the mill pond had gone, as it dipped below the level of the wider Serpentine.

Big House was really called Park House, but Big House is what everyone on the outside called it. May caught up the names on her tongue, "Colonel Barker and Lady Gloria." Singing them as Ma's Cousin Peg Norris did when she came to tea on days off from being a housemaid. Sundays in the front parlour, with lots to report. May thought on how it was the only time Ma sat quiet, her mouth curling at the tips for the best bits, while her fingers worked the cake on her plate into a pyramid of crumbs.

May reached up to feel the bristly edge of her new bob.

"They're all doing it; come on Margaret," Cousin Peg had said one such Sunday.

"All right then, but don't you come crying to me when it don't grow back tomorrow," Ma had turned to May to warn while Cousin Peg helped herself to another slice. Sophie had been there too. Sophie; hiding a smile across the parlour, like she was keeping a secret all to herself.

Big House reared up in front. It had, over time, relaxed down into its foundations like Ma's own ma had done, sitting in her best chair. The lower windows looked half submerged, so that one might easily step up and enter the house through one of these, instead of turning to the door. To the right of the house was Stable Court, and the greenhouses and gardens beyond.

May headed there now, leaving the house behind to pass through the brick archway into the court. It was a large sandy space, surrounded on three sides by stable blocks and deserted just then. Pa's lunch hit out gently against her shoulder as she made her way across to the door in the far wall, admitting entrance to the kitchen gardens.

Inside, all was still. In front of May, the first row of greenhouses cut sharply into view. Through the sloping roofs, May saw tall stalks of green misbehaving, pushing against the glass to be free. She kept on, stepping into the nearest greenhouse. The heat inside was almost unbearable. Rows of gangly broad beans grew skyward, while a few plump marrows fell over their boxes onto the floor. May saw something luminous moving and crouched down beside the leaf. A fat caterpillar made slow progress across its surface. She watched its little body pulse.

"Hello."

May shot up, as one in the grip of some taboo.

"Whatever were you up to down there?" the young man asked.

"I'm looking for Pa."

"In the rhubarb?" He smiled wide, showing a natural space between two front teeth.

Something about it pushed her off-balance.

"I best go," May said, steadying her thoughts.

"Hold on," he said, coming closer. "Who is your father? Perhaps I can help?"

He kept up smiling, revealing more of the gap up close. May thought of the deepest part of the river she hadn't dared yet dive.

"I know you, don't I?" he said, looking at her intently.

"I don't see how." May blushed.

"Yes, you're the little girl from the mill who fell in."

"No, I can swim."

13

"Yes, but you were younger then and so was I. Don't you remember?"

May looked away, feeling her face grow hot a second time against something she couldn't quite get to surface. She sensed him waiting there, expectant for some sudden coming on of memory, but to be called out as girl and little, when she was grown beyond that now, made her forget the very reason for coming up to Big House, stuck standing there with him who had a memory of her she didn't own herself.

"It was at the bridge," he tried again.

"Yes," May said, tracing some outline of recollection now. "But more the river beyond it. I went in for tadpoles."

"And I went in for you."

"I thought it was Pa, but it wasn't. It was a boy." She laughed.

"I must have been about ten. I remember it almost pulled us both under."

"I'd forgotten."

"Your mother made very good cocoa afterwards."

"You met Ma?"

"I came a few times after, before I was stopped."

He smiled, and May did too, bringing it full up to surface now. The black-knowing, of how deep the water sank beyond the calmer mill pond, where it surged and spat to be free of the village. It had almost taken her with it, but then another, stronger than her, had told it no.

"I'm Christopher," he said, holding out a hand.

May took it, wondering if her own felt as smooth.

"Oh, Pa's lunch!" she said, freeing it and looking down for the sack. He found it first, holding it out like it was the first he'd seen.

"Here," he said, giving it over. "For your father, I suspect?"

She nodded and reached to take the bag from his outstretched hand. But she didn't take it, she snatched, thief-like, and pushed out through the rear door to the plot beyond.

14

Mr Berry, the head gardener, stood to one side while Pa and Uncle Richard dug at the ground in front. Her uncle spotted her first and nudged Pa at his side. It was always Pa put in a good word for Uncle Richard when others wouldn't.

"Come to see your old man, have you?" said Pa, looking pleased she had.

May took a good look at his labour. Small earthy lumps lay at his feet, babes on their backs; dried haulm turned skyward like little limbs. Pa was dusty to look at; he always was when working. He had on a pair of wool trousers, turned up at the ankles to show soil-soaked boots. His shirt was rolled up at the sleeves and his tie tucked into this, kept clean there. Pa flicked the tip of his straw hat upwards to reveal the ruddy complexion of a life spent outdoors.

"Well?" he asked May, leaning on the fork, sending it deeper.

"Ma said to bring you lunch over." May tiptoed carefully around the potatoes and gave the bag over. He, in turn, looked to Mr Berry to ask if he might, which May looked from. Pa staked the fork deep, as sentry.

"Off we go then, girl. Care to join me?"

She smiled up at him and everything was right once more. They walked together back towards the greenhouse, leaving Uncle Richard to sup in the shade of the greenhouse wall.

"Why so fast, May?" Pa asked.

"No reason, Pa," May said, keeping pace for both. Inside, the young man was gone, and the caterpillar too.

They reached the courtyard door and went through. The doors of the north stable block were thrown open. A shiny silver automobile poked out, the sun bouncing off its body. The polished funnels and tubing like the organ in church.

"A dangerous thing, May," said Pa, looking. "A man shouldn't ever travel faster than he can walk." He looked down at her. "And a girl neither."

"Yes, Pa."

He tilted his hat back again from where it had fallen,

sending a hand across his forehead. The sun seemed intent on frying everything, May thought, watching a swift free itself from the hot rafters above the car.

A man in overalls appeared from the stable shadows, his face smeared black.

"How goes it, John?" Pa called to him.

John looked up, raising an oily arm to his forehead to shield his stare from the sun.

"Can't get her running, Bob, tried everything."

May followed Pa over to the car.

"I'm thinking of going down to the Croft to ask at the workshop," John told them both, like she had rights to the knowledge too.

"Yeah, I reckon Briggs and Rickards will know. Might be a modern engine but it'll have the same needs as a Marshall, here's betting," Pa offered.

They both straightened up when a young man in a grey suit came towards them from Big House.

"Hello again," he called to her through the gap.

May smiled, wondering afterwards if she'd spoken too.

"Good day to you, Master Christopher." Pa pulled off his hat, polite.

"Yes, hello there," Christopher said, his staying on. "So, you found him?" he asked, addressing May instead.

Pa looked down at her but she lost his expression beneath the brim of his dipped hat.

"Well, Boxton, what do we think? Can we get her up and running?" Christopher asked.

"I'm sure we can, sir, but it might take a little longer."

"Oh well, can't be helped, I'm sure. Georgie will just have to save her picnic for another day," Christopher said, as though they had, the four of them, planned this together.

But, Pa was already pulling her away, back towards the bridge before the outcome was known. They passed the house in silence. Pa dropped her hand and now kept pace. Halfway across the bridge, he paused. He leant against its side and placed both hands face down on top of the flat.

"Have you met the Colonel's son before?" Pa cleared his

16

throat to make the asking easier.

"Just today, Pa," May said, thinking too late of what Christopher had revealed. Wondering why Pa would ask. Hadn't Ma told him about before?

Pa looked downstream, like he was also seeking out the mill, as she had earlier.

"You're a good girl, aren't you, May?"

The question weighed heavy between them, like if it fell off the bridge it would sink to the bottom. May looked up at him and nodded her head in such violent agreement that he laughed, and picking her up, although she felt too old for it, spun her on the spot. When is Sophie coming home? May thought.

They sat down on the other side, finding a large shady sycamore they both approved of. Pa took off his hat and wiped his brow. He had a tan line around the top of his head where it often covered it; like someone had drawn it there using one of Ma's mixing bowls as a guide. He unwrapped the sandwich and gave one half to May. Pa sat back against the trunk and stretched his long legs towards the river. May copied, feeling the springy grass beneath her bare ones.

"How's Ma?" Pa asked.

"Says to bring a couple of prize ones back." She swallowed a large lump of bread half-chewed. "If you can."

He chuckled. "Sounds about right."

Pa unwrapped the now-flattened sweet pie. Cooked blackberry jam spilled out as he broke off the triangular tip, the juice staining his hands, and handed it to May. His fingernails were dirty beneath but it was the clean sort of dirt May loved. He always smelled of it. Like nature loved him, too. She thought of Christopher's clean outstretched hand holding their lunch. For a moment dumbstruck, as though she'd never seen a hand before, or touched one either. Didn't matter, he was the Colonel's son and had ignored Pa.

May swallowed the sweet pie tip. Delicious.

He did have a very nice car though.

SEPTEMBER

"Ma says I'm growing faster than them chicken we raised last Christmas."

"Jan," May giggled, "are you worried you might not make it past the 25th?"

"It's not funny, May." Jan sat up. "Look at me!"

May found it hard to see any change. Jan was Jan, although she had grown increasingly more at odds with herself each time May saw her. May pushed her back down and the two girls laughed, Jan rather painfully, May thought, as though it hurt her to do so. Together, they almost came clean of the wall. May knew something of it too; it was as though their fourteenth year had added an extra season. She pulled self-consciously at her own shirt where the space now lacked, as though to give the new flesh beneath a chance at freedom.

"Perhaps you need work."

"Yes, like you!" Jan said, jumping off the wall. "Can you speak to him then? To Watchet?"

"I'll try." May came off too and cast a glance at the back of the greengrocers. "Got to get back, Jan."

"Me too. Ma wants me to traipse up to Park Farm for eggs."

"Why not send Jimmy?"

"No, I don't mind really," said Jan, straightening her skirt.

May went towards the shop back.

"May!" Jan called after. "If there are any of those broken sweets, like you had last time, I don't mind."

May smiled by way of answer and went inside.

In a slip of generosity, it was Ma who had freed her up

twice a week to help the grocer with deliveries. There was a bike thrown in too, which May kept secret, lest Ma think it too much joy and not serious enough work.

After that first week of turning circles in the saddle at the back of the grocers, May had the hang of it. Out at delivery, she discovered different ways to dream. She peddled at a romantic pace down familiar lanes and byways, which, in her new lover's eyes were rendered changed by darling motion. On the back of the bike, May carried a full box of groceries when out on delivery, bound into her charge with thick string the colour of ink. Ever careful of her new responsibility, May experienced the joy of punching out alone, kept in labour by Watchet long enough to outrun Ma's shadow and the very flesh of her, safely packed in by the mill cottage walls.

Inside the store room, May found Watchet's other assistant, Antony, a gloomy boy some two years older than May. She went over to the crate he packed and peered in. It was a game of sorts, to guess at the destination by the produce. An early blow came when she discovered Ma's order both predictable and mean, while it remained startling just how much sugar disappeared inside Jan's house.

"Not for you, this one." Antony sulked, pushing her back from the crate as though she might rot the veg by looking. He brought down a striped box from a high shelf. It was the colour of sugared mice. "This goes to the house."

May took it, wrapping her arms about its many corners. It was light, despite its size. She read Taylor's Milliners on its top and then a second time, tracing the gold type to enjoy the letters, not caring for the words whole.

"What is it?" she asked.

"I tell you what, wait right there and I'll ask Watchet," he said, leaping over sincerity.

"Alright, don't worry, I'm off." May turned. "Big House, you said?"

"You know another?"

May glanced behind at the box, relieved it held firm after

the sharp turn out of Market Place that joined Park Street. This connected her to the road that ran parallel to the grounds of the park and it was a good fifteen minutes of flat peddling before Big House drive began. She hadn't sought out Watchet to ask about Jan, knowing the answer before then, really: that there was only one bike. May sped clear of the thought, that she might not want to share, knowing Jan, still lost in childish games, would expect it. Somehow, in a fortnight, this new responsibility had become hers. She clung to this independent idea of herself like to the last piece of drift at sea. Her friend deserved better, May thought. But how she loved it, alone, peddling faster now to make it come stronger, to bring the trees to blur like some painter's spent palette until she'd forgotten what guilt was, and in this forgetfulness, almost overshot the gatehouse that met the top of the park.

Inside the parkland, it was the distance again to the house itself. As it came into view from the drive, Big House could have been a mirage, its tall windows reflecting the jagged afternoon sun, as though it hid coyly behind the suggestion of movement in heat. It was irresistibly unattainable, and May reached out towards it, knowing that inside the box behind her, she carried a little piece that would soon belong to the magnificent whole. Eventually, she brought the machine to stop at the end of the drive and climbed off, resting the bicycle against her hip. May caught her breath and with it the oily fresh scent of crushed pine needles that had been present along the fir-lined drive too. She walked with the bike around to the side of the house until she came to the trade entrance. She rang the bell, flicking a glance towards the box as though it might have leapt ahead excited and taken the front door. No one came. She rang again and reached a hand down to try the door. It was locked. She leant the bicycle against the wall and walked backwards, her hands on her sides to press back and glance up at the windows above. This side of the house was more familiar to her, yet cast in shadow now. On the ground floor and away from the service end, a single light stole outwards from a room, illuminating the terrace stones. The gravel crunched as she moved closer.

Inside the room, a man sat at his desk. It was Colonel Barker. He had his head down and was letter writing, the script falling slowly from the pen onto the page in front. May stood transfixed, watching its laboured progress through the corner of the glass until the Colonel hurriedly scooped the papers up and away into a drawer at his side. The door opened and Christopher walked in. May drew closer, feeling how a moth must, watching them talk, knowing she shouldn't. Then Christopher, as though he sensed her close, looked out at May and seeing her see him, waved an arm.

May rushed back to the bike and dragged it away from the wall, leaving bald patches in the gravel.

"Hello again," he called behind, outside now and running to catch up.

"I'm quite sorry," May began, flushing at the fresh thought of it. "I've a box," she pointed backwards, almost dropping the bicycle.

"I've got it," he said, reaching for the frame as it lurched.

May moved apart, so that the bike looked his, and her the one on foot. Remembering the delivery she went back in, reaching down to untie the knotted string.

"I'm just bringing this," May said, trying to make it sound less delivered. "It's addressed to Colonel Barker."

"Yes, it's got his name here," he pointed, smiling at her in that strange way again. "Let's take it in." He walked the bike over to the wall before she'd had time to free the box. May followed behind. Christopher finished off the knots and lifted the package free. "Come on," he said, nodding his head in the direction of the open terrace door.

Inside, the room was losing to the shadows. And while stacked shelves and low chairs gradually became unseen things, there was a visible richness to the air that spoke of lustre and sparkle.

"It'll be for mother," said Christopher, suddenly there beside the switch, blinding her with light. The room was more homely than her imagination had allowed. Christopher dropped down onto one of the low settees and put the box beside him. He looked up at her and smiled.

"Let's open it."

"I won't," May said, grounded by the opposite.

He lifted the lid and went in, carefully bringing out a wide-brimmed hat. It had a pale silk flower sewn to its side and looked lavished upon, as though confident in its simplicity.

"It's not really her thing," he said, turning it in his hands before rising and going over to May.

"It is yours, though," he said, standing back to look.

May froze, lost beneath the brim.

"Good God," he said, turning to reach down into the box again. "Matching gloves!"

"What's this?"

They both looked up. Colonel Barker stood part inside the room, not yet committing to the space where his voice forced ahead. To May, it was as though he caught sight of her before the hat, recognising the former before the latter. She took it off. The Colonel entered the room, closing the door behind him. He went over to Christopher, coming at first embrace-like, to match him in height and more, but ended by holding him roughly by the arm.

"Give those to me," he said, uncurling a ready hand. Christopher placed the gloves into his father's. Colonel Barker released his son and turned to May. "The hat, too," he said.

May went over, offering it outstretched. He looked it over, as Christopher had done, and placed it carefully back into the box.

"I won't tell mother," said Christopher, sounding unsure in it.

"No, don't tell her," mumbled the Colonel, replacing the lid.

May was as close as could be to the terrace opening without being through it.

"You're Thomas's girl," stopped her more as a statement

22

then a question and she nodded in response.

"There'll be trouble if I'm late, Sir," she said, making the Colonel nod this time. She slipped out of the door and back onto the terrace, to fumble for the bicycle and head off, recklessly, into the fast approaching night.

"Big House, you say?"

"Yes, Ma," May replied, keeping to the hall shadows, not committing more person to the room than necessary.

Ma sat eying her beneath the glow of a single lamp. It had been a fast ride back, May had made sure of that. Still, she'd have to return the bike in the morning.

"It's not usual, Watchet sending you there late," came Ma, her needles puncturing the wool in front, driving it up from the ball on her lap. "I'll have words."

"Ma, there's no need," May said, feeling something slip from reach. "There's no danger found about the place and no harm done, is there?"

"I'll have words," Ma repeated, stopping this time. "You been gone longer than most nights and no doubt because you been in mischief of some kind.

"I swear I haven't."

"Ah, don't say a word, I know it, even if you don't yet."

May retreated further into the half-light, as though there were some shame in being seen.

Ma didn't usually chide where work was concerned. She reached a hand to her crown, wondering if Ma saw something there, something that had been, but wasn't now.

"Go up now," Ma said, returned to clicking.

"But Ma, Big House isn't any different to the rest."

"Didn't you hear? To bed with you, girl."

NOVEMBER

It was a full month before May next saw Christopher. It was when the autumn gave way to winter and the first frost began to catch so that the day got drunk on night, filling its sun-time hours darkly, that May's evenings became sunk in longing. Longing for everything that promised light. That everything was carnival at first. It was like the sun, cresting the horizon. A sun that would arrive in six months, but without Sophie driving it forward, even it shone less brightly. It was then that he crept in, filling her thoughts to dance mischief inside her head, until it seemed his weight came equal to carnival day itself, so that she wondered, when the day finally arrived, who she'd come to wear the costume for.

It was a note which came calling first, finding her out at the grocer's.

"You sure that's from your ma?" asked Antony, screwing up his eyes like they might wring the truth from her.

"I said it was, didn't I?" May replied, going back for more paper for the cheese that had already smeared grease all over her hands. She packed the last items into the crate and lifted it, going outside to the bike.

"I'm off, then," she said, coming back inside. "Last one today."

Antony already had his back turned and so she needn't have bothered. Outside, May tugged at the string once more, and when she knew it secure, pushed off.

I didn't mean to get you into trouble, is how the note begun, starting co-conspiratorially enough to set May a fiery blush dancing. *Can you come to the house?*

Can I come to the house? May thought, the answer murky and not fully formed, as she peddled firmly towards Mount Pleasant.

The Mount was a row of grey villas, set back and up from the road so that she had to finish upwards on foot, carrying the crate to get at them. The delivery went around the back, as they mostly did, and May gave it over there, to a Mrs Kelminster who checked the contents while she waited. May stood watching it all pulled out again, thinking how circular it was, but her imagination was soon set to drift by piano keys jumping softly between notes inside the house. It was the sort of sound that suited travel and while she waited, May quickly set off back through the village, because it came easiest to imagine, getting quite far around Milton Street and Mill Lane until abruptly and without knowing how, she had arrived at the gates of Big House. *Can you come to the house?*

"It's all here, I said." Mrs Kelminster had hold of the cheese and barely her patience.

Back on the bike, May thought once more of the note from Christopher. Wouldn't she be a fool to go up to Big House again? She turned in the saddle and looked at the empty box. It promised nothing. May sighed and pushed off, hoping there'd be enough light in the sky to keep foolish things at bay.

Meet me at The Hermitage, Christopher had signed off.

At the back of the park, beyond the tip of the Serpentine, was the place known in the village as the grotto. It was a childhood favourite and one Jan would have longed to claim a secret attachment to when playing was passed. May claimed one now. She returned the bicycle to Watchet's and hurried beyond the mill, slipping through the heavy gate to walk freely towards it. What would Jan say to that?

25

Christopher, this person from this different world, had not been allowed to creep so unobserved into her life, she reasoned. As long as her eyes were open, she would use them to see.

The grotto was more hidden than she'd remembered from childhood, and more secluded too. Covered by a mossy hat, its columns were dressed in a cobweb of lichen. Reaching the first, May put out a hand to run bumpy over its new, unexplored surface. She walked the grotto's length, smiling at its near-return to nature, taking in all of it to record to memory for later, for Jan. It had three arched entrances of equal size and these were exposed to the sky. In its seclusion she was quite alone. May waited until it seemed foolish to wait longer and turned to leave, when someone inside caught her eye. The person there was seated.

"Hello May," Christopher said, rising to join her in the light.

"How long you been sitting there?" May asked, startled at her name on his tongue for the first time.

"Come and see," he said, stepping over the question.

Christopher looked older out of doors; he must have been sixteen or close to that, but had a look claiming more.

"I got your note," May said, sounding cheerful despite herself.

"Yes." He laughed, brightening. "I'm sorry about Father. He's not that frightening, really."

"What did you want to show?"

He walked back inside and May followed. There was something so familiar about him that set her whole self calm. May stopped behind him in the centre of the single room. It was lit from on high by a glassed-over panel in the ceiling. She gasped, unprepared for the strangeness of the place. The walls were covered in a mosaic of shells of different sizes and colours, arranged prettily to fan out and swirl like the movement they'd have practised at the bottom of the sea. There were two stone benches cut into the back wall and in between these, a fireplace, inside of which was the skeleton of an old bird's nest.

"These ones are far from home," he said, going over to touch one of the walls of bright purples, pinks and browns. At his feet a shell had come loose and he bent down to collect it. "Do you ever feel far from home?" he asked turning it in his fingers.

"Only when I imagine I can be," she said without thinking.

He frowned. "Where do you go, when you imagine you can?"

"Parties and places full of lights and people, different people and sometimes so many I can't count their faces and it's always someone different I meet," she said, feeling silly, it all coming full in a rush. "But sometimes I just come here."

"It is nice to disappear, isn't it?" he said. "I'm never able to for long."

"But why would you want to?"

"I suppose you might think that," he said, smiling and looking at her. "Here, a gift." He handed May the shell.

"I can't take that."

"Please," he said, placing it on her open palm and closing her fingers around it. "So you can imagine more easily."

It was warm to touch where he'd held it, making her aware of the intimacy of having it close, and so she opened her fingers, leaving it exposed there.

He led her as far back as the stone bridge and saying goodbye, there they parted. May placed the shell safely inside her coat pocket and made her way back along the grassy bank to the mill cottage, feeling a jumble of joy and despair propelling her forward. This unexpected thing gave rise to something new, in the way that waking up after a fresh discovered dream did. But how long would it last? By the time she was back in her room, leaving Ma fussing in the kitchen below, the shell was cold.

DECEMBER

"Happy Christmas, Sophie," was what May opened her mouth to say, only a magpie, somewhere in the guttering above her window, stole in first with its stark morning caw. The two sisters opened their eyes to each other on this day above the rest, it was usual, but not this time. It was their first apart. It was always May's bed they came to, despite Sophie's being bigger. May missed the chill of the wall against her back where Sophie always sent her, some time in the unknown hours. She nudged backwards to find it now, allowing herself that small tortuous moment of remembrance. There was a gentle knock at the door. Pa.

"Come in," she called.

"Morning, niece, and Happy Christmas!"

Uncle Richard stood in the frame holding one of Ma's trays, laden with hot tea and buttered bread. He was every bit Pa in colour – long days spent side-by-side up at Big House – but in character they divided opinion. Sharp and quick was how May thought of him. A plunger, too. Splashing in where Pa was content to wade. He walked towards her now giving over responsibility for the tray to her legs.

"Thank you," she said, raising herself as far up and out of the covers as modesty allowed.

"You eat up and come down when you're ready," he said, returning to the door. "I'll see to Ma." He winked, leaning back in for the handle.

The door clicked shut quieter than a slipped pin. May looked down. There was something else besides breakfast on the tray top. She lifted the small paper parcel, small enough to be turned between thumb and forefinger. May took a sip of tea and, placing the cup down, set upon unravelling the crude twist of paper. She had almost given up when from its centre dropped a pin, shaped like a seahorse. Its eye was a tiny coral, a creamy pink she hadn't seen before. May smiled, turning it in the fresh new light so it danced on air, as a creature might cresting a wave.

"I told Sophie to come, I did, Dick." It was Ma's voice.

"She's stubborn, like her ma."

"Don't even suggest it, Dick,' Ma said, severing the talk when May appeared. "And don't linger there like you've a right to, girl."

"Thank you, uncle," May said, feeling the weight of new metal against her cardigan front.

"What for?" Ma asked.

"Just a cheap bit of junk I gave her."

"That's where Pa sits," May told him, putting the empty tray down heavy on the dresser top.

"Right you are, May," said Uncle Richard, shuffling backwards in the chair, more like one bedding down than attempting flight.

"Don't you apologise to her." Ma told him. "You're one ungrateful girl." She tutted at the doughy mix, stretching it into submission across the table in front, as though it and May were one and the same.

"Another pot of tea?" May said, wanting to begin fresh. Even if he had found it, a gift was a gift.

"I'll have one if you're offering, daughter." Pa's voice sounded from behind. He lifted her up and spun her round.

"Happy Christmas, Pa," May said, being walked over and dropped heavy into position beside the pot.

The day stretched out plump and giddy, which meant, in Ma's eyes, a successful lunch. There wasn't much left of the day to speak of. The sky black, and resigned to night. May leant, resting against the window ledge and looked out across Mill Lane to the allotment. To its left, the shadow of the church reared up grey, silent and shut, its door barring entry until the next day when it would peel again. Beyond that, each cottage door hid the same scene hers did, she thought, slipping out a sigh.

May lifted her cheek from the cuffs of new red wool and turned from the window to face the room. Ma sat in the armchair, working at the beginnings of its twin, the needles clicking industrially through fresh scarlet. The fire spat modestly in the grate. May rose, going over to drop another log on top. When she did, the flames licked greedily at it. The mantel above was lined with cards. There was one that stood out. A postcard washed by blue that could have been a sea. There was a bright pink lick of paint across its front, like someone had flicked an arch of colour at it. The stroke seemed to dive into the blue. May picked it up and read the reverse.

Ma, Pa and May... Happy Christmas to you three. Love, S.

May warmed her fingers and eyed it again, as she had that morning, and right after lunch once more. *Love, S.* As though to add *Sophie* might make the sender real.

Behind the card sat a postmarked envelope. She hadn't noticed that this morning when the S-card made its debut. The envelope was folded in half, as though hidden first. But there it was for all to see, with the same recognised scrawl on the front as the card, addressed to Ma. May wanted to know its contents, to carry it back to the window seat and read. Find out where Sophie was. And the child, too. Was the other red jumper for her? It was alarming to think they could co-exist so similar, but not know.

"Addressed to you, is it?" came Ma's voice, curling across the room like smoke to meet her there. May knew Ma knew it wasn't, but she looked at the address again, as one whose optimism extended to the impossible. Ma watched still, as though it were a standoff of sorts. May lacked a reply and Ma held the needles.

A row in the street made them forget the letter, and they

both went to the window to look. Outside, Pa lay in a puddle of ice and water. Uncle Richard stood doubled over him, holding his sides as though they might spill free at the next snort.

"They've been at the drink again," said Ma, lifting the net and banging violently against the pane. "IN," she mouthed, releasing the fabric and leaving the room.

Minutes later, May heard the front catch lift and a stream of cold air ran slippery to meet her from the hall. The tip of heat, where the fire licked tall, danced in the grate and then settled when the door was closed. It greeted both men, who shuffled in frozen through the open parlour door, bringing with them the sour musk of spent grain. Pa sank down into the nearest chair.

"May!" announced Uncle Richard, as though she needed welcoming, not him. "Did you two girls have a nice evening?"

Ma's colour rose when he followed this with a lightning-quick peck.

"What's this?" said Pa, unearthing Ma's knitting needles and the ball of red from beneath him.

Ma took the damp wool and glared meanly.

"You too could do with feeding, I reckon," she said, smoothing down her apron front and giving the nod to May.

In the chair Pa dosed, beyond the call of tea.

"And sneak us a drink too, May," said Uncle Richard, tugging at the sleeve of her cardigan when she passed.

In the kitchen, Ma arranged cold cuts and chunks of bread onto a plate. May lifted the cloth from the jug and poured beer into two beakers.

"He's had enough," said Ma.

"Uncle Richard asked."

"Oh, alright then."

Pa woke when Ma put the plates down and then turned up the gas in the lamp to glare unkindly on his features. She left soon after, returning to the kitchen for the rest. May put one of the beakers down where Pa couldn't reach and handed the second to Uncle Richard.

"Thanks, May," he said, taking it and steadying himself against the fireside.

One of the cards had fallen, mopped away by his sleeve. She knew which one and looked about to find it, seeing it eventually behind his legs. He followed her, and placing the empty beaker down, turned his attention to it. He picked it up and read the inscription on the back before turning it front, his eyes flashing surprise.

"That's brave," he said, eyebrows raised.

1935
FEBRUARY

The card and letter both vanished after Christmas and, as the old year gave way to the first fresh months of the new, May found it easier to think less on what was lost and instead on what was certain to come. Carnival.

It was a bleak Sunday afternoon, the kind where church made you sorry to belong and the faces of those familiar sought to irritate rather than soothe. After church and kicking about downstairs beside Ma boiling shirts, May found herself climbing back up to her bedroom in search of something to do.

She paused outside of Sophie's room, the door thrown open as though just departed. Ma had run through it repeatedly with duster and broom so that it looked more guest-ready than a space once lovingly occupied. May went inside and over to the dresser. She picked up the small glass swan which sat there. Ma had polished it so that the gilt enamel of its little beak was rubbed to fade. Where had it come from? A silly gift of Uncle Richard's, May imagined, dismissing broken memory to place it back down again. She turned her head to the window. Sophie had a better view, seeing not just the park and Serpentine, but a corner chunk of Big House, too. May hadn't realised just how much.

Beside the window was a short one-door wardrobe. May went over and opened it, listening for either of Ma's feet on the stairs. There it hung, in front of everything else abandoned, Sophie's carnival costume. The skirt was incomplete; a net of muddy brown under-material that had been planned as a base for feathers. Feathers they'd both collected along the bank. It was the top half of the costume that showed how good Sophie was at needlework; good enough to have won the year previous. Wrapped about the hanger was a thick cotton neck that curled upwards to a small head set with a cardboard beak. The whole swoop of it was threaded with tiny glass beads to give the impression of the animal emerging fresh from water. It was the swan from the dresser, May thought, not making the connection until then. A noise sounded from below, coming on higher where it might meet her. May reached out and pushed the half-finished costume back inside the cupboard before clicking the door closed.

She was back in her room by the time Ma appeared with fresh laundry.

MAY

Carnival day. May sat in her top attic bedroom with needle and thread, putting the finishing touches to her costume. On its way through the fabric, the thread sounded like the regular, shallow breathing of peaceful sleep. Each stitch secured a mossy green pom-pom in place. She knitted her brow and sucked in her bottom lip each time the sharp tip pierced the cream-coloured cotton. It had to be right. A pair of green pom-poms waited their turn beside her on the mattress top. Everything was still. A year gone, almost, and in that stillness, she both missed Sophie and didn't, the costume seeming brighter in her mind's eye at that moment, as one still impressed by life's false vanities. May no longer woke to the late-night creak of the top step and it was a luxury to be the first to the water in the morning. These trivials seeming important then.

Right now, Pa would still be sleeping in the bedroom below, no doubt enjoying the privilege of an hour earned on carnival day, as was tradition. And in the kitchen below him, Ma would have the mixing bowl cupped firmly between breast and forearm, bringing batter for cakes into being.

Inside May's room, the early light brought an undefined glow to the humble furnishings, making them appear better than they were. The bed, with its worn eiderdown, was springy and soft beneath her. When May bent her head to her task, her new crop flopped forward and she reached up each time to tuck hair behind her ears. On the chair near the door sat the four-cornered hat that matched her ensemble, its sides festooned by daffodils with green pom-poms circling the stems. When worn, the hat sat neatly on top of her crown, turning her into a living, breathing spring flower. Sophie's idea, wasn't it? Shame she wouldn't see it done. The thought took May back to that sadness she carried, until the next stitch wilfully returned her to the present. May focussed with a steady hand. She knew the village was alive with activity – could sense it even – and with each careful thread drawn, she was one stitch closer to it.

May looked up at the cover of Nash's Jubilee Special pinned to the opposite wall. At night, with the curtain pulled back, the moon illuminated the room, picking up the lustrous sparkle in the cover model's eyes. Before sleep caught, May had taken to lying on her side to face the deity. It was Cousin Peg who'd slipped her the magazine on her last visit.

"Happy birthday, May." She'd winked, handing it over so Ma wouldn't see.

Her fifteenth, a fortnight gone. It went largely unnoticed in the wake of "you know what" Ma had taken to naming the unnamed thing. What name had Sophie given the baby, May wondered? Where Ma was concerned, May thought better of piping up; of saying the day was rightly hers.

When a birthday card arrived from Aunt Harriet in Poulton, May got to it first and hid it under her pillow. Nothing from Sophie. By the time May had done the sum that proved the immediate crisis had passed, so had any hope of celebration, no matter how small. She hadn't gone looking for it, but instead of resentment, she felt surprising tenderness towards her new niece or nephew. She considered her non-birthday her first duty as aunt.

But this was Carnival Day. For May, there was nothing to match it. For Pa neither, May thought. He loved the Silver Prize Band most. They marched, cheered on by crowds of people who lined the route up Market Place towards Big House, led by Mr Godfrey from Swindon. Last year, Mr Godfrey marched at the front as a painted Red Indian, carrying a tomahawk. After that, the younger boys she knew spent the long days playing Cowboys and Indians in the long grass near Furzey Hill, ambushing each other all summer long. She pricked her finger and thought of Jan, who came moaning one afternoon saying Jimmy had tried scalping.

Pa had played trumpet long before she was born, he said, telling May about the National Band Festival at the Crystal Palace. And when he did, May thought of him as a song bird tuned perfectly inside a glass cage. He looked so smart, Ma boasted, dressed in his best suit. When the men came back, Pa told how all the other troupes had official band uniforms that sung brighter than sound. Ma said it didn't matter, as long as he knew how to blow his own trumpet.

May thought on the fair in the grounds of Big House, with rides powered by the steam engines which moved with red-hot energy, as though driven up from the centre of the earth. Big House, where Christopher would be, too.

"May... May?"

Ma's voice pushed under the door and invaded her space. Pa must be up to make her call so.

"Almost finished," May returned, able to taste Ma's baking that rose up from below.

She pulled the last thread into place and turned the dress the right way. May held it up to herself. There wasn't a mirror in the room, so on a fancy she turned to face the Nash model, mimicking the confident tilt of her head.

"Do you approve?" May asked, blushing at the knowing tone, hers, cutting the silence so freely. She slipped the cotton dress over her underwear and wiggled it into place. May next smoothed her hair with the flat of her hands and reached for the hat. She felt new. Bold even. She opened the door and shot a wink at the wall as she left the room.

May rounded the corner into the kitchen and saw Ma as a stranger might – a country woman, face streaked with flour and rolling pin in hand – labouring away as she always had, as her Ma, and hers before her had too. Upstairs, the Nash model seemed very far. Pa sat in a distant corner of the table, a cup of coffee and plate of bread marking the boundaries of his flour-free kingdom.

"Well, May, don't you look a pretty picture," he said.

She smiled shyly. Ma turned her head, first one way and then the other, like inspecting a prize calf she was entering for the running. "Good. Turn round, let's see the back now."

May obeyed, circling slowly.

"Good idea, that hat," Ma said. "You'll do nicely."

"Thank you, Ma."

Sponges, fresh from the oven, cooled on every possible surface. May looked down at the table where the new mix was being spilled into fresh tins. The air smelt sweet and doughy.

"Are all of those for the tea at the house?" May asked.

"Yes, don't get too close. You'll get flour all over your dress," warned Ma.

"So, May, what are you going to do between now and two?" Pa asked.

"She won't be going outside, ruining it; that's for certain, Bob," came Ma.

"Oh Ma, I'm just getting used to it, that's all," May said, twirling.

She had needed to go. Ma running clean out of lard. May changed and found herself setting off target-like to Watchet's. The sharp poke of the Maypole, darting out from behind the church, was a beacon of sorts and became something to aim for.

May made her way down High Street. It was drunk with activity, blistering energetically in the new day sun. From the turn of London Street, the powerful farm horses came, led out early for watering. May stopped to watch them dip their heads like pistons. The steam engines came rolling slowly after, fizzing with oil. Three gigantic machines, the Fowler, Marshall and the Roller for float pulling. Brake levers came up harshly and the first of the three stopped just short of a drinking shire. May walked on, feeling driven by curiosity to continue past Watchet's, ignoring her task for now. Standing at the corner of London Street and beside the dairy, she saw the petrol depot and smiled. The hand-cranked pumps were hung with garlands of flowers and draped coloured-paper so that the filling station looked Babylonian. She turned back, passing Freefield the butcher's slower the second time. The window was fit to burst with sausages of black, brown and white, arranged to kaleidoscope. Outside the front, impaled with scissor precision, was the prize pig. It watched Market Place, glaring dead-eyed towards the empty pens, like it was contemplating something of being sold and led to butcher. May joined it, looking past the pens to Tom Pax of the Radio and Electrical Supply store. He was up a ladder rigging the public address system. There was the landlord of The Bull below and Pax's assistant, cherishing the bottom rungs. Next door to The Bull was the Reading Room with curtains drawn. Miss Kennings meant to come as something brought breathing from the pages of one of her books. Mary Queen of Scots, talk said. There was bleating from the sheep pens, voiced by a few prize rams on the corner of Park Street, washed down curly-white with ribbons tied to their horns, waiting for Bo Peep to shepherd them on their way.

Inside Watchet's, May told the grocer her reason for coming. His face softened when he realised it wasn't paying she wanted. He lowered his head to continue at finding the brass on the counter fittings, purpling with the effort. In the backroom, she found the lard, cutting an anaemic lump for Ma. May wrapped it in paper and marked in the account book beside Pa, eager to be out of the nothing-dress, keen to get back inside the other that seemed to cast wonder at her body below.

Jan was waiting for her on the corner of Mill Lane. Coming around the corner unseen, May had time to consider her friend's costume. Jan was dressed like the picture of grandma Ma kept on the sideboard. It was hard to tell if the costume was newly made, or had belonged to Jan's own near-ancestor. It was purply-pink with frothy cuffs and a matching hat knotted tight under Jan's chin. Her face looked swollen beneath, like one confined. If ever Jan looked ready to be someone's wife, it was now, May thought, wondering why this idea had come full-flush into her mind just then. Wondering, if turning fifteen produced such thoughts. Instead of this, of seeing her friend as one grown, she wanted to lead her back to childhood, or forward to some other thing, anything which meant not becoming Ma.

"Hey!" Jan called across the lane, waving.

May walked over. Beyond Jan and the churchyard, the urgency of the procession could be heard getting up.

"Jan, what happened to your gingerbread girl?"

"This is more fancy, May, don't you reckon?" She spun, the skirts flaring out like a spinning top. "Yours is just like you said."

May let herself be turned so Jan knew all sides. "Get off!"

"Just seeing off the competition."

"Oh, come on!" May said, pulling Jan towards the rumbling fray, eager to see it set off, one float after another, towards Big House.

When they reached Market Place, they fought to get through the ten-deep crowd to be flush with the front of the procession. Being dressed up, they were let through, May easily and then Jan following, something of a blotch about her face already. A whine, like the feeble call of an injured dog, circled the square each time someone official got too close to the public address system. The crowd seemed to move, and it was like there were two versions of everyone present, one that heaved bodily, neighbour-against-neighbour, and another who sent split-talk whirling around the space, only for it to come back, full-force, in response. It was like standing in front of the mirror and talking to yourself, May thought, both in awe and fear.

"Look!" said Jan with something like envy.

May turned to see a full-skirt, as big as a truck, shudder into view. Above the giant petticoat folds was a corset holding a girl holding a shepherdess's crook. She waved gracefully as she slid past, leaving a dizzying petrol scent in

her wake. Next came a toy box, outside of which had fallen
blocks A, B and C. Out of the A a shabby teddy bear
climbed, and a girl with rosy doll cheeks sat clutching the
C. It kept on past; a tin soldier with a funny walk, a tin army
somewhere further back, a great stack of hay with people
throwing it, a mermaid and a pirate married from the pages
of a book.

May watched, wanting to remember each one. Jan beside
her looked bored, and May wondered how it could be.
When everything, every day, seemed so very not this one.

"Why do you think she's covered herself up, Dick?"

"Probably 'cause she's realised she's nothing to fill that
dress with!"

"Careful, the girl's listening," said Pa.

May looked over at Miss Kennings. Red really wasn't
her colour. Pa shot May one of the smiles he usually
reserved for Ma. In the afternoon light, his face looked more
scarlet than tanned. Pa looked back at his brother and the
two burst out laughing, shoving tumblers together for the
lark of it.

Big House lawn was set with marquees, peaking at the
tips with flags that ran full-drop to the ground. Out of these
spilled the best part of the village. Across the grass, May
caught sight of Ma in the refreshments tent taking charge of
the plum tarts and iced madeira she'd baked that morning.
May knew Ma pushed hers to the front of the stands
whenever a space became available. It was one of the
reasons for keeping distant. The other tea ladies looked on
with something of suspicion but for the most part, put their
energy to collecting shillings for the Cottage Hospital. It
was a good crowd that made it the full route, cheering on
each float as it passed up to the house. Once there, the
horses were untethered and led into Stable Court to rest
beside the big floats.

May pushed ahead to be one of the first to set eyes on the
fair in the grounds; to witness the moment when it still
looked so new, before the crowd sank their heels in or

licked their lips around it. May had grabbed at Jan's hand to weave them through the steady stream of people – some in their Sunday best – others dressed up to the limits of their imagination.

"Werrl arl get there in the end, misses!" A shepherd in a long smock, who'd come as a shepherd from a hundred years previous, shouted. Jan had proved an unwilling athlete, bent over double halfway along the fir-lined drive and remaining there, puffing and blowing out her cheeks while May went ahead. Looking back, May saw her being swallowed by the slow pace of the crowd once more. Later on, she called up to Jan at the top of the helter-skelter, but gave up when she never came down.

"Can I get you another lemonade, daughter?" Pa said with intent.

"Thank you, Pa, no."

"Oh." Pa looked into the dry base of his cup. "How about a slice of cake then?"

May looked up, spotting Uncle Richard over at the coconut shy now, a crowd gathered in a half-moon around him as the wooden balls fell backwards over his shoulder instead of towards the fruit.

"I suppose I might go in for a little slice of Ma's plum tart," Pa said, rubbing his belly to show where it might go. "Support the home front as it were. You'll be alright here for a moment?"

"Yes, Pa," May said.

She watched him travel side-step towards the beer tent where the tart would not be found.

"Let me guess," the voice came softly across her shoulder. "You've come as a plant from the hot house?"

May turned.

"Don't tease her. Anyone can see she's meant to be a spring flower, isn't that right?" the young woman said, giggling. She unlocked an arm from Christopher's to raise a hand to mask it, almost too late on purpose.

"This is Georgie," Christopher said.

He had grown taller since last September when they'd met. May smiled at Georgie, somewhere within which sat a remembered mean thought about a cancelled picnic. Georgie's dress was dusky pink to complement her silvery-blonde bob, cotton-like and finely crimped. May wished her own costume replaced, acutely aware of the stitches which held each pom-pom in place. The hat was worse, weighing heavy like a penance.

"Well, I think you look very nice. May, isn't it?" Christopher said.

"Why don't you tell your father?" Georgie said.

"Yes, I might," he said.

"You needn't do that," May said, loading it with purpose.

"But you must have your chance alongside the others," said Georgie.

"That's enough," Christopher said under his breath, taking Georgie's arm in his grown one. "Well, good luck, May, I like your hat." He smiled, and they were gone.

"Making quite the friends, aren't you?" Pa's voice came thick with drink. He had a full tumbler. The liquid dripped, and he didn't care that he wiped it on his best trousers, trying to hand her a sticky slice of tart. Not one of Ma's. May declined, looking into the crowd again, seeing if Christopher and Georgie were spending time on the other entrants too. Encouraging them, as they had her, but they had vanished.

Across the lawn, a small crowd had gathered around the terrace of the house. Their attention gripped by a table, laden with coloured ribbons, carried there now. The prize-giving. It was what it had all been driving towards, what May, first with and then without Sophie had been getting at. A year back, when they had set about schemes together, she had been sure of it. Now, a year on and it had diminished in her mind's eye.

When May next looked away and back to the tents she caught sight of Christopher with his father. She was pleased Georgie wasn't with him, although it became the opposite when she saw the Colonel take his son roughly by the arm. The pair disappeared behind one of the tents. Without thinking why or what might follow, May went over, Pa being busy with some neighbour or such. She arrived beside the white canvas, running a hand across its tautness and keeping close, feeling that it was a forbidden thing to sneak. She stopped, the Colonel's precision tone came from behind the tent like a stranger's voice, piercing the space, surprised how other it sounded to the man she had come to think of as the best of them.

"She is my concern. Mine!"

"But Father…"

"And indulging her is only making it worse. I forbid you to talk of it again."

May leant closer towards them, out of sight.

"I'm afraid I can't do that," she heard Christopher say with some firmness.

"What's that?"

"I mean to help."

"You'll do no such thing," the Colonel said, his voice thick and on the boil. "Or else you can clear out and you won't see her, not ever."

And there it stopped. May breathed shallow, feeling the day come to mean something else entirely now she had heard it played out in this new way. On the other side of the canvas, the father and son remained silent. Who was to say if either of the two wasn't standing there still, whilst inside the tent, normal things passed other lips, like tea and buttered scones? She turned to see the Colonel pass close by. He didn't stop or even see her there, May thought, realising then, that despite the pom-poms, the best part of her costume was the same colour as the canvas. May peeked behind the tent but Christopher had vanished. She took herself back over the lawn to where Pa now stood alone.

"There you are!" Pa said, jumping, as she slid her arm into his. She led him over to join the growing number gathered about the terrace. Barring those chained to a ride or the drink line, those who could joined them until the crowd swelled. Everyone pushed against their neighbour to see better. May had a good view of jacket backs and best hats, finally giving in to Pa, intent on driving her to the nose of the action. She looked back to check he'd followed, but other parents had taken his place, putting their precious entries alongside her, so that the front row resembled a troupe of flowers, fairies, knights and rural professions in miniature. The terrace doors opened. She looked inside but caught only shadows, like before.

"Let the little ones get a look in," a man behind her flustered. "Oh sorry, Miss." He looked surprised to see her dressed ready. She looked down the line. Was she the eldest? She was certainly the tallest, anchored there. It called up a time Sophie had once tricked her out of a couple of shiny shillings, seducing with a heavy handful of pennies. "Not enough to equal one there," Ma had said, eyeing her up for a fool then. Seemed the trick replayed, May thought, looking down the line.

The crowd closest to the house fractured. A loud bout of shushing pushed back against a round of cheering, inside which, they worked out what was most appropriate. The cheering won out and crashed like a wave through the gathered-many until it roared. May clapped quietly, adding nothing. It brought Colonel Barker out into the afternoon light at the head of a smart-looking set. Amongst them was Christopher and the girl Georgie, arm-in-arm again. They stood to one side, while Colonel Barker stepped forward.

"Welcome…" The crowd roared. "…and thank you for making this our best year. It gives me great pleasure, and even greater difficulty, to judge your efforts," he said.

He buttoned his jacket and May noticed Lady Barker wore the pink hat, blushing to think that she had worn it first. May looked at Christopher, who hadn't seen, appearing cast down then. It gave her something of a guilty thrill to know its meaning.

"This is, I think," he paused, holding them there, "one of the greatest shows in the west of England." The crowd took well, stamping the grass flat around her.

"I have it on good authority," he looked to Lady Barker, "that Mrs Ableson and her two hundred helpers have served their four thousandth tea this afternoon."

May saw her nod.

Another roar came from the crowd, inside of which Lady Barker seemed to wilt.

"I also know," he continued, turning back to address them, "that you wonderful people have been labouring for months now. That everything with four wheels has been closely guarded and locked away, whilst you've transformed them into the marvellous vehicular visions we've seen today."

"First prize to Molly's Toybox!" someone shouted.

"Yes, quite right." He laughed, to show he was with them. "Shall we begin?"

Another cheer. The crowd, set up on drink and feasting, was no longer content to wait politely in silence. May noticed he strained to be heard. Beneath the double set of buttons, he looked a little afraid. Afraid they might throw him over their shoulders and carry him, as one of their own, to the mouth of The Bull.

"The Champion Prize is awarded to…" he consulted a pretty young woman beside him, "…G. Powell's spectacular Horse-drawn Wedding Cake."

Powell stepped forward to take the ribbon and was pulled into a public handshake. A photographer startled the baker, but in a friendly way. It took a long time and the crowd shifted restlessly. Somewhere near the rear a trumpet blew three long notes to accompany Powell back into the crowd.

"Well done, well done," said the Colonel, leaning close to the woman again. "This next award…" He played with the yellow ribbon and addressed the front row. "Well, you all look so wonderful, it could go to anyone."

May hoped it wasn't her. She didn't want it, recognising a building desire to run. To leave Pa, Ma and Christopher, who seemed not to see her now. Confused, to have added him to this equation of loss. The act, however, wasn't hers to perform. A curtain of bodies stood closed at her back.

"But, someone has to win," he said, sure it was true. "Someone whose costume truly captures the spirit of this great day."

May closed her eyes.

"The prize for Outstanding Solo Dress is awarded to… Mabel March." He bent down as the little fairy, willed on by her parents, pushed herself across the grass. The streamers danced on her tricycle, even when the photographer snapped them to blur. The crowd let out a collective coo.

"Well done," he told them.

She walked off in the grip of her mother's hand, the token pinned to her front. Her father carried the trike.

"Now, I said it could go to any one of you." The silk of a second yellow tapped away against his mouth. "And in truth, I meant it."

The woman whispered in his ear.

"We felt there was another who captured the essence of this day, no, this season." Colonel Barker looked at her. "Who we couldn't let escape."

The colour left May's face.

"May Thomas, our spring flower."

And flooded back so fast she thought it might pop.

"Go on, May!" Pa shouted, pushing his way to the front. May remained rooted and everyone, including the Colonel, waited. At last she drifted over, almost falling into his outstretched arms as he pinned the badge to her front.

"That wasn't so bad, was it?" he said. Up close, he was out of focus and unrestrained. He spun her around to face the crowd. The flash replaced each of them with a thousand little dots. Pa led her back, but had no intention of leaving and found them a good spot at the thick of it, where the people she knew, her folk, poked and pulled at the place where the ribbon sat pinned to her breast. It was only when she looked up, did she notice Christopher, grinning right at her.

"Hey Ma. Ma!"

"Not so loud, Pa, she heard you," May whispered,

47

turning back.

"Ma!" he cried again. The crowd dispersed. Across the lawn, Ma was talking to an unknown woman, in the height of some mood. The woman stood quite still, hands neatly clasped in front, making Ma seem more abstract by comparison.

"Ma!" It was unlike Pa to persist, but he did. A passing pair turned and giggled. "Come over here, woman, won't you!"

Ma curtseyed at her companion before taking leave. May watched her come, thinking that the day went beyond the blush.

"My goodness, woman, am I speaking French?"

"I heard you, Bob, you don't need to shout. I was in a conversation."

"Well," he whistled through closed teeth, "don't you sound fine."

May looked at him, missing the man who turned potatoes, preferring Ma right then.

"If you must know, Robert, I been talking to Mrs Flaxen."

"Mrs who?"

"The housekeeper. She's after my plum tart recipe. Says her ladyship was quite taken with it."

"Plum tart indeed! May here won a top prize." He pushed May in between them and she went. Pa pressed down on her shoulders to steady himself.

"That true, girl?" Ma asked.

"Yes, Ma, I won it."

Ma looked down at the ribbon. "Well, I never." She paused. "Now that's done with, run back to the house for the other tart I made this morning. It'll be on the table."

"Take this, Pa," May said, relieving herself of the hat, and relieved to be going.

"Don't be long, now, go the back way," Ma called after.

May crossed the lawn and headed off in the direction of the Serpentine. When she reached the bridge she looked back. In the distance it was Pa she noticed. He had taken off his hat and was wearing May's, dancing a jig in front of Uncle Richard.

The bridge was deserted on the far side. May sensed the fair follow her up until the boathouse. At first, she thought a couple had snuck down there on the opposite bank and she steered her gaze away, before she realised it was the shadow of laughter and the odd rising note caught in the acoustics. The bar of metal holding the ribbon, tapped all-knowing.

"Damned fool," she said, tugging at a pom-pom. She had won, though, but this, mixed with regret at feeling too grown to enjoy it, cancelled out the joy.

May reached the gate. She pulled it open and there she remained, for standing on the iron-railed bridge, was Christopher. He leant over the side, dropping cigarette ash into the water. His head hung heavy, close to the iron. The door gave her away, creaking loudly on its hinges, too heavy to hold part-way open for long. He heard it and looked up.

"May." He flicked the cigarette into the pool and straightened up.

"Come to have a good laugh, have you?" she said, letting it slam after all and walking over.

"What?" He registered the ribbon. "Oh yes, that."

"In case you weren't aware, I'm not a child."

"No, I can see that," he mumbled. "I mean, of course you're not."

A duck quacked below and they both leant over to look at it.

"The swimming must be good here."

"It is," she said.

"I hate just driving past."

"I don't see why."

"Well, I can't go in. Everyone can see you, for one thing," he said.

Christopher quickly set his gaze on the water in front and May blushed deeply seeing him do it.

"Where's your hat? I thought they'd give you a crown."

49

"No, Mabel must have got to it first," May said.

"Oh, you could have beaten her."

"She's five!" May giggled, swinging back on her heels.

"If I did something foolish, would you hate me?" he asked serious.

"Depends, can you swim?"

"It's just, a chap like me doesn't often get to do the things he would like to."

"I'd mind you don't ruin that nice jacket."

"No, quite right." He took it off and hung it over the railing. It looked like it was about to slip in and May put out a hand to steady it. Before she knew what was to follow, he had hold of the hand and her too. She was conscious of the ribbon squashing against his shirt front but was happy for the intimacy. They separated and looked down at the fallen jacket which had drifted out into the centre of the pond, its arms spread wide like it was swimming.

"I'll get it," May said, going over.

Before he could protest, she was over on the far bank, wading in. When May came out, some of the larger pom-poms stayed behind and floated like lilies.

"Thanks," he said, smiling.

"That's alright," she said, handing it to him.

"Won't you catch cold?" He reached out again, unsuccessful this time.

"No, I'll go in now," she said trying to make it sound normal, as though words were the only thing to have touched her lips.

"Goodbye then, Queen o' the May." He grinned.

"It's not nice when you tease."

She walked past him and towards the mill cottage gate without looking back once. It was only when the gate was closed did she turn, as though the kick of her heart could open the catch and fling her, arms-wide, back into his.

The back door was open when May got to it, and beyond its threshold, was Sophie. She sat at the kitchen table and there was a child on her lap. It slept and Sophie put out a finger to silence May, as though anticipating the first to speak would be she. Her nails were red tipped. May's eyes fell on an open leather envelope on the table beside Sophie. The contents were strewn across the surface. These included a letter with an ornate signature and enough pound notes to fill a lifetime. When she saw her looking, Sophie disturbed the mess, stashing it into the holding absolutely. One or two of the notes took to the floor and May bent to pick them up. Sophie took them back fast to join with the rest. She dropped the envelope into the open suitcase at her side.

"Thank you," Sophie expelled at last.

"Can I see him?" May asked.

"It's a girl." Sophie said, showing the little face blanketed by wool. The snub nose wrinkled somewhere in the depths of sleep.

"Oh Sophie, she's beautiful! What's her name?"

"Honor."

"Honor. Hello Honor," May whispered. "I'm your Aunt May."

"Still not bothering to change before you go swimming, then?"

May looked down at the drenched half of herself. "I had to rescue someone who fell in."

"Who? I didn't hear anything." Sophie sat up, alert.

"Someone who'd got carried away by carnival spirit."

"How was it, then?" Sophie said, pressing against the chair back.

"Alright. Weren't the same of course."

"Don't be silly. Bet I weren't missed much."

"Can't believe you're back. Does Ma know?"

The baby hiccupped and they both looked.

"Course she knows; I wrote her," said Sophie, her arms a pendulum with the child as bob. Honor wriggled and readied her mouth, like a conductor holding the first note.

"You go get changed, May," Sophie whispered.

"Yes, but please, when I come back let's sit down and you tell me all about where you've been. I want to know everything."

May sped from the room taking the stairs two at a time.

The child wailed below. In her room, she threw off the sodden costume and grabbed at the first dress in the cupboard, a brown checked one, but thought better of it and pulled on a lemon coloured skirt and white shirt as best she could. It had fit perfectly well last summer but it was the best she had and it wasn't clear who this day might yet produce a second time. She sat down to lace up a pair of white plimsolls. In the bathroom, May washed her face. Bits of pondweed had crept into her parting and she pulled them out along with a few real strands, wincing. Honor had quieted, sleeping no doubt, and so May took her time, brushing out her bob in front of the mirror, making the damp strands shiny and new again. She searched her reflection for any sign of change, feeling strangely let down.

Back on the landing, May slipped down the stairs quietly, not committing a full foot to each step. Honor was a good child and to think, she had seen her first, before Ma perhaps. May wouldn't keep any secrets from Sophie, though. She needed a confidant. It'd be the first good thing to get them back to where they were. Show Sophie she didn't hold it against her, her leaving without a word. She would lay her secret kiss down like a peace offering.

May rounded the corner. The kitchen was empty of both Sophie and her little caravan. If the chair hadn't been pulled out different, it might have been a dream. The back door stood wide open too. May ran out into the garden, her mind running further, searching for any sign Sophie had simply gone for air. Nothing. Just the garden as it ever was with Pa's old shed at the end, refusing to crumble. She opened the side gate and went out into the street, searching both ways. There was no one to be seen on the village-side, or on the bridge where Christopher had been but wasn't now. He was gone then, and all of a sudden came a feeling of being left behind, like coming last to a joke. Maybe Sophie was on her way up to Big House? Why had she stayed by the mirror so long? She ran back into the house and looked for the plum tart. Sure enough, it was on the table where Ma had said it would be, only there was a slice missing. A great big one. It would have to do. May found a cloth and covered it over, pulling the door shut behind as she hurried back up to Big House.

"Where the hell have you been, girl?" Ma's eyes searched like pokers. Pa stood quietly at her side, rubbing his head. Ma grabbed the dish and lifted the cloth on one side.

"Good, well, at least you brought the right one," said Ma, calmed for now.

She put the cloth back over the complete half. May scanned the crowd, thinner now as the day drew to a close. A woman whose outline seemed similar held something up to a man in front.

"Sophie!" May shouted.

"Shush, are you feeling right in the head?" came Ma, through teeth.

It was a toy bear. Not Sophie, with a child, and a suitcase, and all that money.

"What have you done with your ribbon, May?" Pa asked, looking at the spot that missed it now.

The pond.

"More to the point, Bill, why's she changed?" Ma said. "It's not a catalogue show. You haven't given her none of that beer, have you?" went direct to Pa.

Pa stared still at the vacant spot and May felt a blush rise on the skin beneath.

"You've got trouble in your eyes girl, stay there," Ma commanded, going off. "You too," she called back, pointing at where Pa might also.

"What a day," he said.

"Sorry, Pa," May said carelessly, knowing the day meant something different to him than to her.

"What for?" he asked, looking down at her, waiting.

She choked up a sob in the silence he placed there, making free with the wetness that flooded her cheeks. It was seeing Sophie with Honor and then not seeing her again. It was being robbed of a kiss, but then stealing one freely back. It was owning all this knowledge, but instead of being richer for it, feeling poor all the same. It all came out now without warning, her head buried in Pa's jacket sleeve where she found comfort in the smell of old tobacco and home. Pa held close.

"I know, I know," he said.

Ma came back towards them across the lawn. She no longer held the tart. May thought she looked lost without it, pastry or some such bake being something of a prop of hers.

They joined the last of the troupe on the main drive for the walk home. Ma insisted they went the proper way, as though any other was worth less. Ma looked like Pa's straight shovel had found her back, like she was born to higher things than them. May sighed. To have gone by the Serpentine instead would have meant avoiding the lewd chat of those far-gone.

"Didn't you win? Cumon, petal, gissa kiss," said someone, coming close.

"Ignore them, love."

"Thanks, Uncle Richard, I mean to," May said, focussing full-stare on the distance.

And looking there at the unseen, May thought on Sophie and how much Ma and Pa knew. It was like it hadn't happened, and the thought of it as something imagined made May want to run mad shouting it was true so they all heard. So they all believed. So she didn't have to feel so blessed and so crazy all at once for having both Sophie and Honor in reach.

"And I said, 'I hope your ladyship enjoys this as much tomorrow as she did today,' I did." Ma spoke now.

"I bet you did, Ma, I bet you did."

"Then, Bob, guess what?"

"I can har—"

"She looks at it and lifts the sheet and there's a slice gone."

"A whole slice?" Pa looked down at May, who walked on silently.

"Yes, I'd only rested it down for five minutes, but that pesky kitchen lad, you know, Jenny's boy John, must have whipped it out good and fast and stuck it in his pocket, no doubt." Ma paused for breath required. "She says she's gonna have words but will serve it nonetheless, seeing as I went to the trouble to go home and fetch it."

"Suppose she'll just cut it up first, ain't that right, Ma?" Uncle Richard grinned, winking at May.

"That's probably exactly what she'll do, Dick," said Ma, animation returned. "Thank you for the suggestion, I ju—"

The deafening cry of a horn drove them all off the road like cattle. May landed on two feet in the ditch beside Pa, while Ma held on to Uncle Richard on the opposite bank. May watched as Georgie and Christopher sped past in a motorcar that threw up the road in its wake.

Ma, Pa, Uncle Richard and May regrouped behind it, shaking the dust from their clothes to continue on their way.

"I'm almost glad there ain't enough to go round," said Ma.

They were all of them early to bed but only May late to rise. She dreamt of a giant swan and her on its back, gliding as one down the Serpentine. In the dream, May wore a crown that drowned her view each time it fell. The water was still, like nothing played beneath. After time, the swan stopped swimming and drifted towards the boatshed. There was someone inside but May couldn't see who, only felt fear at knowing. The swan drifted closer but the person in the shadows looked more lost, not coming clear at all, although inside the shed she could see the detail on the hung rigging and the pulleys used as winch. May yanked hard on the swan's neck so it turned away, only wondering then who it was. She looked back and woke up.

"May? May, come downstairs," Ma called up from below.

May pulled a cardigan off the chair, and slipping it around her shoulders, went. She looked in the kitchen; no Ma. The kettle steamed on the hotplate with the cloth still wrapped around its handle. May heard muffled voices coming from the front parlour. She pushed the door open. Inside, sat Ma and Pa with a police officer.

"May, this is Constable Green."

May pulled the cardigan tight.

"Come and sit down, please, young Miss," he said.

She did, in the seat he offered. Ma was next to him on the sofa, while Pa had his back to them over by the front window, more out of the room than in it. She wished she'd have been told to dress first, feeling exposed, almost more truthful, in her nightgown. The room seemed emptier, despite them being gathered there.

"The Constable's here to—" began Ma.

"Perhaps it's better if I explain, Mrs Thomas, if you beg my pardon," he said, knowing something of Ma already.

"Yes, of course," Ma mumbled, refilling her teacup.

He turned to face May. "There's been some money taken from Park House, yesterday, during the carnival."

May looked at the biscuits Ma had spread so they fanned on the plate.

"You listening?" said Ma.

May looked up.

"It must have happened in the afternoon, because Colonel Barker remembers Mrs Ableson handing him the donations for the Cottage Hospital just before the prize giving." The officer looked at his notebook. "These, he then proceeded to lock in the safe in his study. He remembers once, and only once, leaving the envelope on his desk while he was called away momentarily, then returning to put the same envelo— sorry," he flicked through the pages, "soft leather case with a button clasp, inside the safe."

He looked at May, as though now, on cue, she might produce a notebook of her own and begin reading. Ma had the crumbs of a biscuit around her mouth and was gulping tea back faster than she could pour.

"On closer inspection this morning," he continued, "the Colonel discovered it was not the same case, although it had done a good impression of the first, the contents of this new one being completely empty. And the money, two hundred and fifty pounds, gone."

"Oh, tell her the worst of it, Constable," said Ma, seizing her chance to make free with words.

"Your mother here contacted the station this morning with news that another robbery had taken place."

"I walked round there myself before I was dressed," Ma said.

"To report the theft of a number of household items," he continued, something of a blush at his cheek.

May looked at the mantelpiece. Now she knew why the room was so spartan. The small clock was gone, as was the silver-plate tea set which usually sat, unused, in the cabinet at its side.

"Not just them, May," Ma gestured, following her gaze, "but Pa's best suitcase from under the bed, Grandma's gold ring and the tin full of change from on top of the dresser." She looked at the PC. "It's not much, Constable, but to people like us it's a damned sight more. Add to that the tart dish I'll probably never see again and it's a pretty bleak picture."

"Yes, well, it's a big coincidence, wouldn't you agree, Miss?"

She did.

"If that's what you say," May said.

"Your mother tells me you came back here after the prize giving – congratulations, by the way."

"Thanks."

"Didn't see anything then, did you?"

"Only that the back door was open, I think."

"And you didn't think to say nothing? You stupid girl," said Ma.

"Open, was it?" he wrote. "I'll need to check it for signs of forced entry." The PC rose.

"There ain't any." Pa's voice joined them. He turned, looking at May.

"In that case I won't bother," said the PC, sitting down. "Were you here by yourself then, Miss?"

"Yes."

"You see anyone before you come in here, May?" Pa asked.

"No, Pa."

"Not near the bridge?" Pa came again.

"No, Pa," she said, feeling her face a beacon.

"Well, I'll be in touch if I hear anything." The PC rose between them. "I'm sorry for your loss, Mrs Thomas; it's a mighty great shame for the hospital, too. I hear that's what keeps it running."

Ma led him from the room. Pa looked at her still, and when they could be heard faint at the door, he spoke.

"I came looking for you 'cause I was worried," he said, clearing his throat. "At first, I thought it was some girl from the village."

Sophie. He must have seen her.

"I wondered if it was the drink playing tricks on my eyes. But then I got to thinking, why you were so long in coming back." He paused and seemed to prickle, remembering. "Pushed up against the bridge with the Colonel's lad, I didn't…"

May blushed. He saw and looked down, as though this confirmed something in his mind's eye.

"I guess leaving the door open didn't matter to you then." He turned back to the window. "Just you was gone an awful long time."

"It was shut, the door was," she tried.

"Didn't have you down for a liar, May."

"It was just kissing, Pa."

"You and your sister grew up together; you were bound to tread the same path."

May opened her mouth to speak but lost sense of what should follow. This thing he thought he knew had roots. These would grow still, binding themselves to what was once. It wasn't true. Christopher had played her for a fool, like she was a child still. Was he Sophie's friend too? Her tongue choked on the words needed and she swallowed them down hard, along with everything she knew was true.

That Sophie and Christopher had acted together. How could she tell Pa? Bring Honor in when the money was taken for her? That it was Christopher who was Honor's pa. How had she not seen it?

"Well, don't look so upset, Bob, it's only a suitcase," Ma said, entering the room again. "All my finest things gone. Not to mention the money for the hospital, what a terrible thing that is on top. I wonder if they'll hold the carnival next year." She tidied away the tea things. "Robbers in our midst taking our most precious things like they've a right to 'em."

Pa stayed there, silent, turned against them both. When May finally left the room, the hall looked off. She caught her eye in the mirror and wondered who it was looking back.

JUNE

Past Furzey Hill lay the old Saxon burial ground. May liked to go there and lie on the hillocks left behind by the mounds of peat driven upwards. It was here she lay now, on a day hotter and more furious than any Fairford had known that summer so far.

Since the day following carnival, it was hard for May to be anywhere near Pa when he was so distant. At least here, the distance was real, and for a time she could forget the pain of the last month, seeing him turn from her at table, or pass without wishing the day good. Ma noticed nothing amiss.

"You becoming a hoity young Miss," she muttered each time she caught May quiet. "Nothing like me as a young woman," always following.

To get away from it, May thought, was as good as holding breath as long as a duck. Here, she was alone and could pretend all was as it had been before that day that robbed her of everything dear.

"You," May said, finding herself covered. She raised an arm to see the owner of the shadow that mapped her middle.

"The May Queen," Christopher replied, bowing deeply so that the sun hit her full in the face.

"Oh, bugger off." May pulled over her shoes to buckle.

"Don't go," he said.

She looked up and he smiled. So this was the face that caught Sophie? May passed quickly through liking so she might be freed up for hate.

"I imagine you come here a lot," he said, looking around. "It's nice."

"I won't anymore," said May.

"It's peaceful."

He had a white shirt on, rolled up high in the sleeves, not like Pa's, May thought, but tucked neatly, turn-after-turn as though folding them was his sole occupation.

"You don't go outside much, do you?" said May.

"No." He brightened, looking at his forearms. "I suppose I don't."

She remembered something of being held and bent her head to her shoes, letting her toes find the ends and slowly setting the clasps to work. Christopher left her, going over to a nearby tree. He set about climbing a low hanging branch, some three foot from the ground.

"You go up there, you'll fall," May called over.

"Would you care if I did?"

"Up to you what you do."

May watched as he jumped, hooking first one leg and then the other around the wood. He pulled himself up with strong arms into a sort of sitting position on the flat of the ledge.

"Easy," he said, getting up to standing height.

May looked up, her breath catching. It was as though he had turned giant. This gold headed almost-man had grown taller. His arms were now a vibrant green, turned so by the leaves above and beside him, as though they celebrated his presence among them. He looked over at May.

"Why don't you come up?"

It seemed bolder in the asking than that time on the bridge, when Pa had still cherished and Sophie's baby was only the idea of one, and she, May, hadn't lost them all.

"No," she said.

"You might one day."

"What does that mean?"

"Nothing," he said, sitting down again. It was his turn to look lost to shadows and it was enough to hold her there. But it was all she could do, standing quiet, sensing danger in more.

"I'm expected back," she said at last.

He looked up and smiled. It wasn't as bright as before.

61

"Goodbye, May," he said when she passed.

"Come here!" Jan sat up, alert to let her voice be carried. Across the open field, the dog came running. When it reached her it fell, tongue exposed, towards her face.

"Enough!" she giggled.

May watched on, leaning back on the grass. It was two days since meeting Christopher and seeing him climb the tree but the image of him standing there, a finger curled to invite her up, hadn't faded. She held out a crust of sandwich and Dorry filled the space with a single bite.

"What you thinking of doing, May?" Jan asked, giving over a small bone-end from her pocket. Dorry settled intently at her side, getting to work.

"I'm busy with the rounds."

"You telling me you going to ride that bike forever?" Jan brushed the last crumbs of sponge from her lap. "Around the village?"

"Course not, silly. There's something freeing in it, though, Jan, like it's natural to have purpose beyond them four walls." She gestured towards the mill.

"Aunt Doris wants me to go up to the house but I think that's dull."

"Get married, then."

"Me! Do you think you will?"

"Ma says she feels sorry for my husband."

"Oh May, your ma is funny!"

They cleared away the wrappings and walked, with Dorry following, towards the mill.

"Come in for tea and we'll talk more about your husband, though," said May, smiling.

"Don't you say anything more, May, I swear it."

Ma wasn't in when they arrived. Jan, shuffling clumsy across the stone in the kitchen, drew out a chair and watched Dorry through the open backdoor bite at thin air, trying at flies.

"Can he have some water?"

"You want tea too?" May asked, gesturing down at a low shelf where the bowl still sat from their last visit.

Jan went over and let the water fall heavy from the jug. She bent and mopped the spill with her sleeve before taking the bowl outside where the dog wagged approval. Over at the stove, May turned the top plate hotter and set the kettle on top.

"Perhaps I wouldn't mind a husband," said Jan, picking at the tablecloth end.

May pulled cups down from the dresser and found spoons.

"You got someone in mind?"

"No." Jan coloured.

"You do!"

"If I did, you got to keep shut," Jan said, looking up. "Not a peep to your ma."

May studied the face in front, wondering when it had paired her with Ma. She sighed.

"We ain't that close, Jan."

"She's your ma, ain't she?"

The kettle whistled fiercely and May went over, bringing it carefully back to the table. She let the water spout into the ready pot and returned it to the cooler grill.

"Either say or don't, Jan. Be careful, that's all," May said, sitting.

"I ain't stupid like…"

"Like Sophie?"

"I didn't mean her."

"Don't matter if you did; she was, really." She put a spoon into the pot to stir up the leaves and replaced the lid. "Pass me your cup." It came over and May set about pouring through the strainer.

"His name's George if you must know," said Jan after her first sip.

"George Motkins, from the farm?"

"Yes!" Jan said breathy and thick.

May sipped lightly at her own cup, regarding her friend. In the silence that followed was the moment needed to open about Christopher. To tell of the kiss at the carnival, the shell house and Furzey Hill. Even more important though, to pipe up about Honor and how Honor belonged to him. This thing she knew that would knock George Motkins into the next county. But instead, Jan went on, telling how she walked for miles to meet George, this thing they did and that thing they longed to, her eyes coming to a dewy stupor the more taken by the idea of him, and her with him, she got. May listened and sipped until her cup was dry, not having lost a word of her own.

"He made me promise."

"Promise what?" May asked.

Dorry came sounding between them, registering a bark sharper than the kettle's peep.

"What's that dog doing here?" asked Ma standing in the doorway, holding a bag of shopping high to her chest.

"Sorry, Mrs Thomas," said Jan, tripping to get at Dorry.

"Wait there, Jan," said Ma turning to catch her. "You might want to hear this, too."

"You want tea, Ma?" May asked.

"Keep your tea!" Ma collapsed into the chair left out by Jan. "I've come from Mrs Adson. She says her Harry came back from the house this morning. Guess what he heard?" She drew breath, grabbing at the pot and pouring messy into Jan's used cup. "Only that Colonel Barker's upped and left. Got himself a fancy woman!"

"Poor Lady Barker," said Jan.

"Yes, what an embarrassment. Fine folk ain't free of it, and sometimes it comes worse for them, them being some way along in the world already."

May poured into Ma's drained cup. The tea had stewed itself a dark, treacle colour.

"Did she say anything else?" asked May.

"What else is there?" Ma scolded. "We'll hold up, May. Ain't Pa's fault he's working for a broken man."

Jan gasped and shook her head with fresh virtue. May was reminded that Jan had a secret too.

"You best run home and only tell your ma what she need

hear," said Ma. "May, we'll start early. Pa'll want a good dinner after this shock."

It turned out Pa didn't feel as much as Ma thought proper, and Ma, watching him for any sign of distress, became more so herself when none arrived. She sulked about for weeks following, as though stranded on the moral high alone with no hope of rescue. Bits and pieces of news tripped from Ma's tongue, fresh back from the village when she went looking for it. Telling how Lady Barker had shut herself away, refusing all visits from friends and the well-meaning, turning all cars around as soon as arrived. And the son, Christopher, packed off after the Colonel. Sent off up the vast fir-lined drive in a car of his own.

It was when Cousin Peg came for tea next, that May found herself sitting, listening intent to the back-and-forth.

"It's the lad I feel sorry for," said Ma.

"Yes, he's troubled, though. No doubt he's seen some of it over the years."

"Peggy, whatever can you mean?" Ma said, lamb-like.

They both turned to May, who looked eyes-busy to the magazine on her lap.

"You've got to swear not to repeat it," said Cousin Peg, stealing a final one at May.

"She ain't listening," said Ma, leaning forward.

"Well, often a night, there's been screaming heard."

"Oh Peg, no!"

"Only it's mostly her screaming, he just gets angry and barks orders. And once I seen her all puffy from crying so much and with her face swollen." She ran a finger beneath her left socket. "Here."

Ma sat back. "There was always something about him I didn't like," she said.

"Margaret, you haven't heard the half of it," said Cousin Peg.

Ma looked at May. "Make a fresh pot for Cousin Peg, please." To May it seemed they held breath watching her leave.

"Uncle Richard!" May said, finding him slumped over a chair in the kitchen. She filled the kettle and emptied the pot leaves into the bucket.

"They still at it in there?"

"They are," said May.

"I knew of course," he said, taking a pipe from his pocket and tapping it on the table end. "Pulled the wool over most eyes, including your Pa's, but not mine."

"Suspect Pa was working," May said, meeting his stare.

"You don't come with his lunch anymore, do you?" He struck a match and lit the tobacco, puffing it meanly.

"I'm working, too."

"Yes, I know, with Watchet." He took the pipe from his lips and pointed it at her. "If he gives you any trouble, you tell me, alright?"

"Ma should know you're here," said May, going to the hall.

"No, no need," he said, rising. "Just brought this on my way, passing." He dropped a large, wet paper package onto the tabletop before tugging on his jacket as though to right it, though it was long past that.

When he had gone, May went over to the table and put the chair under. The parcel was soft to touch, with the muddy end of a tail fin poking out. It had stray tobacco fragments stuck to it. She picked them out and dropped them into the bucket. The fishing was good at Park House. Uncle Richard never learned, though.

Lying in bed that night, May's thoughts turned to Park House and Christopher. She thought about the time on the bridge, when Sophie had been close by, too. That was a meeting of sorts, perhaps a plan was formed then and she had come racing between them with her fool's errand. Had the kiss been to distract? To give Sophie time needed? May rolled out flat and stared up into the ceiling's blackness where the tender welt of a bruise came to mind, imagining she saw an eye above. It seemed to penetrate and pin her there. A weight of knowledge hung suspended in its unflinching pupil. May flipped over, if anything, to get away from seeing too much.

JULY

Curiosity and something not yet known as longing brought May next to Furzey Hill. The curiosity came first, and it was bred of need. Of needing to see if she might climb the tree as he had, curling her limbs around it to reach such heights she'd come to think of as belonging to him and his kind. Thinking, that it didn't matter if she were fifteen, if for just one moment she could get above the bark to glance upon the landscape through the canopy.

Longing came next, but not with its name. May knew enough of feeling to be aware of its presence, but had not come far enough in grown thought, to marry it to its namesake. Christopher had played on her mind a good while longer than he ought to, creeping in like the wind to make the true day blunder. It was Ma always brought her back to ground when she caught May intent on the unseen. Ma brought them all to ground, May thought, as she pushed up the mound to get at some unknown, lighter thing.

It was a couple of days since Cousin Peg's visit, with the news of Christopher's flight behind his father's, and a full two weeks since they'd met. May pulled at the long grass she passed, freeing handfuls as she pressed onwards. She clenched her fists to force stopping and sighed heavy, if anything to make her breath come regular, trying to return it to its unheard self. Instead, she had the idea that it worked against her, speeding up so that everything inside beat like the wings of a hundred butterflies trapped behind a net. It was unnerving to not know one's self she thought, stripping the seeds from a fresh plucked barley straw. And a bad thing, to want to have this one small spoon of pleasure – to sit on the hill's top and think on he who she should call brother, if he were good.

When she thought of what Sophie had suffered, May ran conflicted against herself. What pain he had inflicted upon Pa, too, for playing against both his daughters. Should she think unkindly of Christopher? Yes, she must. It was for him Sophie had left. It was for him she had lied. It was for him Pa turned. What was it drew her onwards then? Her very self went one way and then the other. It was like trying to unpick a rotten knot, looking like it might come free, only to find another tie to unlace. It sent her heart spiralling miserably low as she reached higher ground. Then, as though forced to start again, May forgot which side was good and which bad, for standing on the bough of the hill was he.

"May!" Christopher said, coming fast paced to her side.

"Why aren't you gone?" May asked, finding herself turned.

He laughed, resuming something of his previous air. This time, it made her want to reach up and score a point for Sophie. "The car's over there," he said, nodding in its direction. "I'll be away soon." His eyes flashed an idea. "Would you like a ride first?"

"We're not like you," May said, meaning only herself.

"I suppose you heard about Father then?"

"It's only talk," May said.

"That's the thing, May, it isn't."

"You admit it, then?" she asked. In his face, she saw defiance and hate, but destined for someone other than her. He blinked it away like it never had been and looked full of a fresh idea. Taking her face in his hands, he kissed her again. It went on longer than the first and May wondered after if she'd struggled enough.

"I'd like to see you when I return," Christopher said, freeing her.

"After what you've done?"

"They already think I've left," he said, walking further off. "But I had to arrange things."

"What things?"

69

"Don't say you saw me," he called, reaching the car and climbing in.

"More lies," she shouted in vain, sending a hand up to her cheeks where they burned hot and cold. Her voice must have reached him as the engine caught, because with a hand raised high, he was gone.

Nothing learnt and more taken, May thought afterwards, resting her toes in the shallows of the mill pond. Her heart flipped manically as the moment itself came real again; as precise as a papercut. She pushed her heels deeper into the mud bottom where it was cooler still, anything to set a frost at such remembrance. A finch, high in a tree, called to its mate to say the nest was ready. May looked over at the mill and thought how Ma might worry if she was much later out with no purpose. It was the home she had and was once Sophie's too and that meant something. Sophie. What would she say? May was afraid to own it. What did he want from her? She blushed fresh, thinking that through the unlikeliest of circumstances, she had been caught twice. And through this, he'd become something new to keep quiet about, to not let Pa see in her eyes, and to not ever let Sophie know what she'd done. May pulled her feet free and rose, carrying her shoes, to finish her journey barefoot, across the bridge to home.

"Pass the butter please," May asked of Ma at table that evening.

"You back terrible late, May," Ma said, sending it over.

"I been with Jan," May said in the same time it took to remove one slippery curl.

AUGUST

It was funny how the absence of those around her, including Jan off busy with George Motkins, made May consider her own lack of engagement. There was Watchet's of course, but the more her understanding of the countryside around Fairford expanded, so her excitement for it contracted. It was as though its beauty had a limit and the more she saw of it, the more threadbare it became, leaving her imagination craving richer things.

It was soon after Christopher's departure from the hill, that a new thing inside May took shape. It was the idea of him as unreachable that meant he became something new to aim for. Christopher existed beyond the lanes, and no matter how hard in her mind's eye she peddled to grasp him, the further he sped ahead. It was as though the act of kissing him twice had signed and dotted some physical bond between them. It was a bitter contract, she thought miserably, walking the bicycle back to the village along the Welsh Way with a puncture up front. It was time to return to Watchet's now the last order of the day was done. The sun was a distant memory behind, making skeletal shadows of both May and the frame at her side.

There was something else Cousin Peg had said on her last visit. Something dark and set in shadows too that had its beginning up at Big House. This, tied together with the day of the last kiss, left May wondering if the two were related. She experienced something like guilt. Wondering if her own actions were in any way bound to Lady Barker's unhappiness. Had Christopher's going away anything to do with his getting too near to either Sophie or herself? More so Sophie. Definitely Sophie, May thought, feeling in some way responsible for any actions Colonel Barker now administered.

A figure approached waving and for a time May ignored it, head down, taking clean green breaths of the hedgerows as she passed. In the sky, crow-sound cracked rhythmically with the turning click of each wheel, the front one wheezing like the end was near. The person came closer and May recognised the oversized hat and short, punctured walk, more suited to entering rooms unheard with silent tea trays than travelling country lanes. Cousin Peg outside of Big House was a different being. She had already begun conversing before reaching May.

"You know how I get, May," Cousin Peg finished, answering herself. She stopped to lean back against the steep incline of the bank.

"Shall I walk with you home?" May offered, thinking she might leave the bike behind if that were to happen.

"No, no, just give me a moment to catch breath and then I'll be on my way."

May steered the bike to the opposite bank and rested it against the hedge there, coming back across with a small paper parcel of ham and bread from the basket.

"Here." She tore a chunk from the bread, trying as neatly as possible to make it a clean cut, and offered up slices of the meat next.

"It'll do for later," Peg said, taking the lot and rewrapping it into one crude lump. "I get a lift most days, as you know, but John Boxton ain't so free with his time these days." She took off her shoes and rubbed one foot and then the other. "Always busy running errands for her, like a man half his age!"

May stayed silent, thinking fresh about Lady Barker and the fighting.

"Don't you go into service, May. Look how we all have to suffer."

"I hope it isn't too terrible there."

"What you heard?" said Peg, eyes meeting May's side-on.

"Nothing, of course."

"Best you don't gossip, May, it ain't right, only…" She puffed sharply, confusing tears with air. "It's been so hard, getting caught up in it. That boy, no help sulking about the place when he visits and his pa, the worst of them." She drew out a handkerchief and blew. "Lucky your uncle's around to calm him somewhat."

"Uncle Richard?"

"Proper thick they are. But he knows his place."

Cousin Peg said nothing more on the subject of Big House, asking instead how Ma got her sheets to starch so crisply and how the pastry came to crumble so lightly. Neither of which May had the ready answer for. They said their goodbyes and May continued onwards, leaving her in the lane wiping her skirts down, the parcel of food under one arm and handbag occupying the other. It was impossible to think of Uncle Richard having anything sensible to do with the Colonel. Business concerning the gardens would go through Mr Berry first and then Pa after, May thought, feeling disappointed Cousin Peg didn't know this too. What crazy ideas she had, mixing truth with serial stories from her best magazines. When May next turned, her cousin had made faster progress and was at the brow of the hill, looking more a wild blotch on the horizon than a relative heading homeward.

1936
SEPTEMBER

"You ain't nurturing enough to help 'em on."

"Bob, you can be master of the land up at Big House but this little patch here, let me."

"You don't want to listen to reason," said Pa.

"I think my older brother don't like being told what's what."

"Have it your way," Pa looked up, "but they won't last."

This went back and forth across the eight by twelve allotment for the best part of the morning. May sat listening through the open parlour window. She flicked through the pages of the magazine on her lap without reading and pulled the shawl tight. The pair outside broke from arguing, falling silent. A stalemate she'd seen before, knowing the outcome even if Pa didn't. At their feet lay Uncle Richard's latest scheme, a crop of strawberry runners, the foundlings still in some doubt as to their end. Pa stood facing the Coln as it battled downstream. Uncle Richard faced Pa still but May watched him cast a glance opposite to the great window of St Mary's. From inside the room, May could hear the river flow fast, pushed on by an unchanged wind.

"Ah Dick, I'll help you if you be so intent on growing them," Pa said, turning to speak first.

"Good man!" said Uncle Richard. "If only you'd have said sooner. I've got an errand due but can see to helping later."

"You mean I've been idling all morning?"

"Not idle, brother. Now I know you care for me as much you ever did." He went in, embrace-like, but Pa moved quick.

Uncle Richard opened the gate and set out in the direction of the high street, leaving Pa and the dug plot. As he passed, he shot May a wink so that her gaze dropped. In the room, the clock didn't chime. Time was one of the things taken that hadn't been put right yet. Its absence on the mantelpiece revealed a tear in the paper which curled upwards without resistance. Outside, Pa began the work. A pile of peaty soil laboured upwards beside him. She watched him go steady but hid in the corner of the frame, should he look up and spot her now. He bent to his task, laying first one and then the next infant shoot, spacing them regular. Something must have made him laugh because a smile danced across his face.

A year and more gone and when May spoke to Pa at all now, it was like a shadow descended to mask his joy. They moved around the house like two long passed, as though the memory of something good was all that kept them turning.

"How long you gonna sit there looking so morose, girl?"

"I'm not morose, Ma, I'm reading."

Ma entered the space proper and slid the duster the full length of the mantle, with the satisfaction of one unhindered by worldly goods.

"Same thing. They still out there?"

"Just Pa."

"Another hare-brained scheme of your uncle's, is it? I almost feel sorry for him, not having a wifey at home to keep him straight. But, who'd have him hey…except me?"

"No one, I imagine."

"You run outside and tell Pa dinner's ready. And close that window."

Pa looked up when she approached, but leaned further to digging when he saw her, filling the fresh gutter back up to surface height.

"Pa," she whispered. "Ma says dinner's ready and to come."

"Half hour."

May stood for a moment, feeling like a blunt spade when

75

he didn't offer more. She turned and walked back to the cottage alone. She was surprised how quickly she'd taken to it. In earlier months, she'd dreamed up ways of pleasing, putting time into the scrub, the wash and the beating at carpets until her arms hurt, but nothing came of it, except material sparkle.

"We might make a good little woman of you yet," Ma had said, getting some joy at least.

And why not? Acceptance of any kind was something.

May closed the front door and returned to the parlour. She fell down deliberate over the arm of the sofa to stretch out its full length, overcome by how wrong it all was. How it still wounded. She slid her hands beneath the seat cushion below her head and that's when she felt it. The crisp, exact touch of paper. She freed her left hand from beneath the foam, bringing with it, clutched between index and middle, an envelope; and it had been opened.

It was addressed to Ma in the same, childish scribble she knew from countless birthday cards and smuggled notes past. It belonged to Sophie and looked freshly written. What had it been? One year and more since that time at carnival when she had laid eyes on Honor and it had seemed a good thing she had. Then there was what followed, with Christopher, that had chased her in thought down the months like a borrowed dream. She hadn't told any of it. Not to Ma, or Jan, who came visiting now with George Motkins pinned to one arm. May rose with her find, returning to the chair beside the window. She looked across the road to where Pa worked on still. She pulled out the single sheet of light blue paper and read:

You best stop begging me, Ma, because I said before, I ain't coming back, not ever…

"You even been and told him dinner's ready?" said Ma, sticking her head into the room.

"I'll go now," May said, dropping the magazine on top,

thinking Ma could as good read the rest on her face.

"You can't; he's gone," said Ma looking outside. Pa had. "Come then, Uncle Richard's something for you in the kitchen, though heaven knows what."

May waited until Ma had gone ahead before rising with the letter. She stuffed it into the sideboard on her way past.

Sophie wasn't coming, May thought, stumbling as one cut towards the kitchen. She didn't want any of them and Ma knew. She must be set up proper on what was taken, May thought, and by him. Inside the kitchen, Ma busied herself laying plates and cutlery. Uncle Richard sat at the table, a large brown paper parcel in front of him.

"Can you guess, May?" he said, tapping its top.

"Thought you were in the village?" she asked.

"He won't tell me, you wicked man!" Ma swiped out with a cloth.

"Margaret, you've had three tries now; let May take her turn." He turned the shape to face her.

"Go on, girl. I'm giving you three goes."

"Firewood?" she said.

"A log for the fire? Do you think I'd wrap up a log for burning?"

"A birdhouse, then."

"Have you no imagination? These be modern times, girl, think!"

"I don't know, I'm sorry," May said, landing them in silence.

"Very well, you two country lasses," he said, bringing Ma to bubble. "Prepare to be amazed." He tore the paper off. It was a wireless radio.

"Oh Richard, it's beautiful!" said Ma, raising the towel to muffle what shriek remained.

"It is, ain't it? What do you think, May?"

What did she?

"May, answer your uncle."

"It's lovely."

"It's for you, May. Call it a late birthday present."

"Very late I'd say. That's a little much for the girl," said Ma, swiping him again but harder.

"Nonsense, Margaret; her sixteenth? It's second hand, anyhow; the Colonel gave it to me, and now I'm giving it to May."

"Why'd he want to do that?" asked Ma.

"Reckon I'm useful about the place."

So the Colonel was back?

"Come on, May, have a look," he said.

May stepped forward. Through the coat of shine, it managed to be both brown and black. She reached out to the grill shaped like a half-moon to let her fingers bump down the groves.

"Bakelite, May," he said, following her progress. "This you twist to get the needle to move, look." He demonstrated, moving the pin back and forth. The grate crackled as it travelled through the stations.

"This one's for the volume." He showed. "Then alls you've got to do," he opened the back and pointed inside, "is take this here accumulator battery to Pax's to charge. Might need the wheelbarrow for that, though; it's heavy. There, got one!"

May leant in close. Out of the scratch came the rich quiver of a woman's voice. Her song ringed smokey through the space. May reached down to turn the knob until the treacly notes came higher.

"What's she singing about then?" Ma said, leaning across the table.

"Her lost love," he said, taking hold and spinning her around the kitchen so that they didn't notice when he entered.

"You can hear that to the end of the village."

Ma and Uncle Richard broke apart. May stood back against the sink as Pa stepped across the room and reached around to the switch.

"That what you been up to while I been sowing, Dick?"

"It was a surprise, Bob, for May."

"What surprise?" asked Pa, fierce and desperate all at

once.

"For her birthday, Bob. Late present. Ain't that kind of him?" said Ma.

"Can't an uncle treat his niece?"

"I don't want her idling up in her room. The answer's no, I'm afraid," said Pa, pulling himself tall.

"Oh Bob, really," Ma said.

"It'll have to go back, I'm sorry."

May stayed quiet.

"Thinking on it, Bob," came Ma, travelling different. "It could sit where the clock used to in the parlour. Then Dick can see it when he comes round."

"Margaret…"

"It's second hand, they won't take it."

"God almighty, have it your way, woman!" Pa cried, walking from the room. They all heard him take the stairs.

"He'll be the first to it each morning," Uncle Richard said once Pa was clear of them. "Just you wait and see, Margaret."

"And your Ma didn't say anything?" Jan rolled over onto her belly, kicking her heels freely against the wallpaper.

"No, Jan, I told you, remember?"

"And now you can't find the letter?" Jan dug her finger into the bag of sherbet and vacuumed off the sticky red crystals in one.

"I'm only telling you, Jan, so keep quiet, alright?"

May rose and opened her bedroom door; silence. Pa was up at Big House and Ma was in the village. Perhaps it was tucked neatly into her apron strings. Ma must have thought it strange, turning up like that in the sideboard. The letter had vanished a week ago.

"Point is, Sophie don't want to come back, Jan." May said, closing the door. She dropped back down onto the bed. "She said it, she's forgotten about me; about him."

"Who's him?" Jan asked.

"Pa, of course."

Jan folded the edges of the bag down and held it open for

May, as though it was the right thing to do.

"Thought you were watching your figure?" May said, licking her finger and covering it with sugar.

"George says I'm fine as I am," said Jan.

May felt the sour tang of cherry fizz on her tongue. The taste, reminding her of simpler times, was good.

"What else does George say?"

Jan flicked up onto her heels. "Only that we're to be married!"

"That your secret, then?" May asked.

"Don't sound too excited," Jan confirmed, grinning. "My life's finally coming good."

"If that's what you think," said May.

"It's what my ma thinks, I'm sixteen and not getting younger."

"I hope you're happy with George, that's all."

May smiled and wiped her sticky finger on her skirt, wondering if it was too soon to know full-happiness, to really understand its like, especially when they were still eating sherbet.

Jan dropped a fresh piece into her mouth and swallowed. "Imagine if we found someone for you too, May!"

DECEMBER

May looked up at the window. Alone, each cut piece of glass meant nothing. But put together, the shards formed a composite whole, which in turn was part of a series of twenty-eight frames, reading like a giant's picture book around the church. In front of her, four slim panels rose towards a central arch. The left held a green figure snaked around a tree while the first woman leaned in curious. Next to this, the double bay was filled with a white-hot bush of fire beside Gideon and above him, a man meant for an angel in flight, looking near to this imagining once a day when the sun came to pass behind him. On the last panel, the Queen of Sheba offered up a casket of sorts to Solomon while three kings looked on.

May idled here, so that the stems in her hand grew hot and then limp. She placed the last of them into the vase on the table below the scene. Winter jasmine and viburnum, chosen that morning by the vicar's wife, gave off a sweet scent like bottled perfume. There was something unholy in it. It looked well though. The tiny yellow flowers of the jasmine formed the backdrop against which she fanned the cluster-like petals of the white and pink shrub.

It was Ma's idea she switch Watchet for worship. Offering up her daughter's services in front of the best part of the congregation, the vicar's wife couldn't refuse. To May's relief, Mrs Hunniford looked pleased she'd offered. Quitting the two wheels she'd come to think of as hers still left May cold, her place filled by a boy half her age. It wasn't right for a young woman to gallivant, Ma reminded nightly, intent on this one crusade, before May relinquished and the battle was won. Now, she had to content herself with serving up front in the shop and this – changing the flowers for service once a week and more so at Christmas time. May sighed. Fairford Church had been going nowhere fast for hundreds of years and wasn't about to speed up now.

There were small joys to be had, though. This next window was her favourite; it was earlier in the story, when the world felt new. Before all those famous figures, saint-this and king-that, climbed up and crowded into the narrow spaces to stake their claim on perpetuity. She stood back. The arrangement looked the best so far.

The main door to the church closed heavily. Quite early for service, May thought, gathering up her things, not wanting to be found there. She looked up. An old woman slipped into a pew in the main aisle. If recent sermons were anything to go by, the village had long outgrown the interior. Despite this, customs were maintained and the front two pews remained Colonel Barker's, whether he'd come for mass tonight or not. The rest of the congregation, penned in on holy days, heated the old place so that when each of them opened their mouths to sing, it was with enough warmth of feeling to melt the lead from their cames.

May gathered up the last of the stems, enough for the final arrangement in the Lady Chapel. Here, the altar cloth was bare and in need of colour. The milky white figure of its namesake was carved asleep beside her last husband, their hands closed, fingertips spearing skyward in precision prayer. She looked up. Winter's light blanched the glass above. The smallest shard was the babe himself. May took the vase over to the bench closest the effigy and sat down, setting it carefully on the space beside her. She slid backwards and laid the foliage out, sorting it first by type and then height. She heard the echo of the woman's footsteps as she left, chasing real ones back along the aisle. Then the bench behind her creaked.

"Your hair's grown out."

May looked up. Christopher was suddenly so present, leaning in from the pew behind, that she confused it with what a vision might be. In the time passed between them he had changed most, she thought, with a jaw of cut stubble spread from one ear to the next and hair worked into a style new to this place.

"Just goes to show how long it's been," he said for her.

"I never told anyone," she said.

"What about?"

"About Furzey Hill," she said, suddenly blushing, remembering the kiss and knowing he'd think of that, too.

"Those pink ones look too cheerful to be winter flowers," he said, reaching a hand over to cover hers.

"They're viburnum," she told, freeing it and sending the bunch held rushing towards the vase. "They grow in summer, too."

"Then I will think of them all year round."

"Why are you here?" May asked, wanting distance then, thinking of Sophie.

"Father's back."

"You come with him?"

"No," he said and then after some time, "Do you still swim? At the mill, I mean?"

"It's not heated."

"No, of course not. I feel sorry for the ducks!"

"Surprised you can see them, speeding past as you do."

"Actually, I sold the car," he said, leaning in further. "Had to pay a debt."

"What a shame!"

"Mother told me you stopped coming up to see your father."

"Been busy," May said, holding the vase up. A little pool of water ran to the back of the pew.

"Will you be here tonight?"

"We always come to service," she said, placing it down. "Those of us able."

Christopher nodded and looked to May like he thought on taking her hand again. For Sophie, she told herself, she hid them beneath her.

It wasn't until the door closed and he had gone that she remembered breathing. She looked at the display, as though she'd worked in a stupor the whole time, moving someone else's hands, not hers. May walked over to the altar and placed the vase down. The spray of yellow jasmine outnumbered the shorter viburnum three stems to one. They did make you think of summer. She teased out one yellow stalk and then another, snapping them in half when she had a big enough bunch. May worked her way back around the church like this, in a mood of high-colour and confusion, until only a sea of pink remained.

"Not there, closer to the front." Ma shooed her onwards. The church had already filled nearest the altar, the congregation listing towards the point at which they deemed His power strongest.

"Ma, this'll have to do."

"Very well. Move along, quickly now!"

They shuffled sideways past friends and neighbours and dropped into the empty seats. May was squeezed in tight next to Ma and the warm haunch of another ma entirely.

"There's Cousin Peg." Ma said. "Don't know how she got so near the front. Ain't Christian to push."

"No, Ma."

"I hope Dick comes," said Ma looking.

"If he comes," her father said from two over, "he'll stay near the back. Lucky man."

"What's that you say, Bob?"

"He'll come."

"May!" Ma's hands went towards the biggest display on the altar, a sea of pink and white. "Didn't the vicar's wife give you anything other than that old shrub to work with?"

A member of the choir reached up to light the candle at the end of their bench and Ma turned her attention to this. As the light caught on down the pews, the space looked even more luminous and the people too. Like grown-up cherubs, their cheeks ruddy from the sting of winter. Some of the men dozed, fighting the coming of the midnight service, and were nudged awake by their womenfolk.

"May, May!"

She turned. Jan waved wildly from two rows back, George Motkins at her side. May smiled and when Jan sent it back, her face dimpled. May turned to face front; the pews there were empty still. It wouldn't start until they'd come. Everyone waited expectantly. The crowd bleated on, sounding an ungodly riot, growing fat on gossip as they strained for any news of Colonel Barker. Was it true what had been said? And would they, who could judge, be able to tell if it wasn't?

"Some say it's the boy." May stiffened, hearing Ma tell her neighbour. "He's troubled."

Yes, thought May. When the congregation seemed like it could take no more, they came. Colonel and Lady Barker went arm-against-arm down the nave as though nothing had ever come close to touching them, nor ever would. Following behind were Christopher and Georgie. She wore a fur-trimmed cape, moving against her shoulders with something of the animal who had worn it first. She had grown more beautiful, May thought, to match him.

"Look at her, Lady of the Manor that might be," Ma whispered in May's ear.

May undertook a detailed study of her palms. When she next looked up, she caught only the backs of their heads. The choristers were the last to dip and the congregation stayed seated for the sliver of a second, before the organ sucked in its breath and exhaled sharply. They rose as one into the fanfare.

"Please be seated," Reverend Hunniford said after the first carol. "Merry Christmas, all. I see many friendly faces here today and when we look back at the years passed, we can say with certainty, these have been trying times. Times we have all met with fortitude and a willing heart. Amen."

"Amen," they chorused.

"Let us give thanks to the saviour of the Cottage Hospital. Long may it continue thanks to the anonymous donation it received."

"Amen!" someone sent front.

"A good thing from the ashes of bad," he continued. "We must pray that the almighty gives us the strength to forgive the greedy and look upon those lost souls with a kind heart and an open door."

"Easier said when it ain't your door," Ma whispered.

"Before we begin the first reading," he continued, "I would like to announce that in the new year, I shall be leaving you all." The church drew in its breath. "There is a parish in a poor part of London in need, and like one of His flock I am driven on."

"Amen, Reverend," came someone new.

"Let us rise for the second carol, In Dulci Jubilo, and then Colonel Barker will honour us with a short reading."

While everyone in the room eyed Colonel Barker, raised above them on the altar step, May caught the rise and fall of Lady Barker's shoulders. It was impossible not to wonder, while he enlightened them with bright tales of hope and forgiveness, if he had given a similar talk back at Big House, making them all stand to attention as he did now. It was when he spoke of infidelity and lust, that the congregation shuffled uneasily and May's attention drew upwards.

"He's a nerve," Ma said, puffed up fit to burst. But it was Christopher who May saw looked the most affected. It was he who had played Sophie and her for fools, deserting one and then the other, who looked so awkward for the hearing of it said. The lesson was for him and the congregation, though slow to take, knew it too.

When the speech was finished, the crowd stood and cheered, stamping their feet, thinking they were back at carnival. "I've never held much stock by what Peg says," said Ma above the fray.

Colonel Barker, cast in the glow of the tall candles around him, looked washed new, May thought, and rightly so.

"A very spirited reading, sir," the reverend said,

reclaiming the lectern. "The First Noel, please rise."

May did, blindly, like one called up.

"The-urr furrr-ust no-ow-well..," Ma sang, eager, as they all were, to rejoice in him returned.

May stood in silence while they unified in song around her. So, Christopher was cast out, too. What they thought they knew, that the Colonel had acted to clear up the wrong of a wayward son, wasn't the half of it. Did any of them know, right now, that Sophie and Honor were lost still?

She looked up at the central image of the glass sea and fishing boats stuck there, before looking over at Christopher, hemmed in by Lady Barker and Georgie. He wasn't singing either.

PART TWO

1940
MAY

"May, May! Come, sit here!"

"Move your hat, then."

Jan did, the navy beret skirting her fingertips mid-air before May descended.

"I joined for that," Jan said, despite the danger passed.

"You best keep it on your head, then."

The two enjoyed giggling, which soon became a fit of more. The other girls on the bus turned to stare until Jan stopped sombre and May did the same. George had been one of the first, somewhere called Luttange.

"Can't believe it's finally come," May said soft.

"It has, hasn't it?" Jan sniffed.

Finally. May had hold of the small purse, one Sophie'd left. It held her bus ticket, WRNS Letter and the lipstick, a relic from Sophie's dresser. May had smeared the stale tip on a piece of tissue so it regained some of its sunset cerise. The bus driver counted the berets before sitting up front. He called up the engine, giving two blasts of the horn freely to those outside sweeping farewell handkerchiefs through the air. Ma was there, blowing tears into hers. May looked past but it was only women who'd come. Most of the men had left already, and those who'd stayed behind had their hands full, like Pa. She leant over past Jan to raise a hand for Ma, but felt shy suddenly and held it static. The other girls sat up on their knees and waved theirs wide-armed at loved ones. When the bus pulled away, some of them fell backwards against the seat cushions and laughed.

"Yours looks better than mine," Jan said through thick-rims. May looked over, the blue jacket strained against her friend.

"I tell you what. When we arrive, I'll put a pleat here." May pulled at the material gently until Jan's eyes wrinkled beneath the frames.

"What will it be like, May?" Jan asked, relaxing.

"Like nothing we're used to."

Most of the girls had removed their hats, revealing tight curls pinned back. May did the same and pressed her hand firmly around her head to check the grips held. She undid her jacket buttons and sat back.

London. Imagine. Basic training first and then, who knew what? Assigned to a division once they'd seen what she took to. Someone near the front laughed and it was like a bird chirping, the sound bouncing contentedly back to their row. Did any of them know?

"Can you type?" the recruiting Wren had asked. "Have you qualifications?" May thought she'd failed right then, but the letter landed on the mat, as though it always knew it would.

"Goodbye, goodbye!" shouted someone at the front as they met the end of the London Road and turned out of the village.

Jan kept up a good wrestle with her uniform until they disembarked in need of petrol somewhere on the edge of London. The driver got out and the Wrens all stepped down to smoke. A tall girl joined the group, proving popular when she offered cigarettes from a pack. Jan came back over to May with one barely lit and the two shared it leaning against the warm metal where the engine was.

"What about them sailors, hey?" said Jan.

"If they haven't left already," May said. "Free a man for the fleet, remember."

"You think there won't be any?"

"Just mean don't get too attached. Easy come, easy go," May followed, wishing she hadn't. It put silence between them. May thought of Christopher then. Wondering even now if he'd signed up, been swallowed like everyone else. He hadn't been seen much. "Off getting educated, and he needs it," Ma had said, like it might have been medicine. Or paying to keep Sophie, May hoped.

It surprised her, how war crept along the country lanes and found them so soon, curling its fingers over the thatching and raising up window sashes to take what it wanted. Who it wanted. "Don't matter if you're the baker's boy or Lord of the Manor, it ain't fussy like that," Ma said as though she knew, had known, all about it. Going on to croak about Uncle Harry who really had known, before any of them.

May heard rumours of Christopher going, cursing herself every time she stepped outside for lifting her ear skyward, in case some fragment of news nicked the air. News which might lead to Sophie, but unable to ask. Aware that talk spread fast. Faster than the droning propellers overhead, going to set up at the base that wrecked the farmland to the west. The one person who would know what went on at Big House was Pa. And she'd lost him, too. Christopher had followed, and news of Sophie and Honor with him. It was the same dead conclusion she reached each time she thought about it. It came again now and she blew the loss away quickly like smoke to inhale again fresh. A sharp liquid smell from the tank stung her nostrils instead. That's how it was to be now. It wasn't for May to worry whether Christopher lived or died. She crushed the stub beneath her shoe and climbed aboard.

Entering London, the bus sped past rows of tall terraces dripping in cornicing like iced cakes. Every time it looked like they might miss a turn, the gearbox grated as the driver corrected it. It jerked them all to one side, pushing foreheads and flat palms white against the glass as they leant towards the city beyond, willing themselves out, or it, in. Like caged birds, they chirped and fluttered until the bus finally came to rest beside a great brick building caught somewhere between a hospital and a school. It occupied a whole corner of the street and was flanked on the left by a smart brick block. Across the road was a cosy looking pub and a neat row of terraced cottages, like home in purpose May thought, but otherwise not. May sought out the tiny mirror from her bag and positioned her hat carefully over the pins so that it sat at a tilt.

"Do mine too?" asked Jan.

"You know, we might not be in together," May said, leaning over.

"You worry too much."

"Course I do." May smiled. "There, you're done."

"You two got return tickets, then?"

The driver was in the aisle beside them. Outside the window, the other girls were filing into the building. On the pavement, two lonely suitcases kicked about. They dismounted and laid claim. May gripped at the handle of hers like it was Ma's gloved one and climbed the Wrenery steps.

"Ah, country reserves, we're saved!" sang an officer descending the hall stairway. Above her, it snaked up and into darkness. She carried the tricorner hat of her rank and stopped on the bottom step. She grinned like one winning, wanting it seen she had the advantage. Her uniform fit glove-like and was a world away from the coarse jackets and skirts lined up in the hall. May's skin itched beneath the thick of her stockings. Silk, she thought of the other. When she looked up, the officer had sight of her. May thought on how it was like being back in the mill garden at night with one keen predator looking back. Another officer entered the hall. This one was cut from a different cloth, covering the short and wide of her. She stood below the first, her back turned to them who waited there. Then she spun and the first officer pointed, leaving May in no doubt at whom.

"You. Step forward, please."

May did.

"Name?" she asked. "Come on."

"May Thomas, Ma'am."

"Thomas," she said. "I am Officer Jenkins and this is Petty Officer Shaw."

94

Shaw sniffed to show it was she.

"A question," shrilled Jenkins. "Do you think it's acceptable to alter an official uniform?"

The other recruits drew breath. May shook her head, wishing she was of the flock.

"In the navy," Jenkin's sighed, "gestures of the head are only used on combat submarines." Her eyes pinched. "Are you going into battle, Thomas?"

"No, Ma'am."

"Good. Although it's not good, is it? Not good at all."

May looked down at her uniform, thinking opposite, and of the hours it took to get it this good, like Sophie had taught.

"Take it off then," said Jenkins, finally brought to pounce.

"Excuse me." Shaw coughed. "There's no time, Ma'am, drill starts soon."

"Yes, and we run a tight ship, don't we?" Jenkins said. "See to it that Thomas changes it back."

"Yes, Ma'am."

Jenkins looked at May like prey escaped and clicked down off the bottom step. When she was gone, Shaw squared off, pulling the stub of a pencil from her breast pocket.

"Back in line, Thomas, and change it today," she said, licking the blunt lead before running it down the clipboard.

"Parker, Rhodes, James and Bartlett," she shouted. The owners assembled in front. "Room 4G. Top of the stairs."

The four named made their ascent, dragging cases after.

"Next, Brown, Bates, Thomas." She looked up. "No, Thomas, you wait there," Shaw pushed the space in front of her back in line. The stub found another two. "Crawley, Jones R." Jan stepped forward.

"4H, same way as the others." Shaw threw a thumb over her shoulder. "Pay attention."

Jan was the last to climb and tripped looking back to find May. The other three giggled.

"You four." Shaw pointed. "Wallace, Jones S, Adams and

Thomas." They stepped forward. "10G for you lot. Top of the stairs and right, then up the next flight and so on." She licked the stub again. "Don't mind if the siren goes off, bound to happen one day soon and you'll be the first to know!"

May joined the three others for the climb. The tall smoker from the garage was one of them. Below them, a fresh group of Wrens punched through the main door.

The cramped half of the attic assigned to them contained four put-up beds, a worn chest of drawers pushed up against the only decent wall, and windows cut into two corners. May looked out of one as a pigeon took flight from a chimney stack. She took the only bed not yet claimed and sat, the springs expired long ago. They were in the attic and in a strange way, it felt like home.

"You gonna unpack that thing?"

Ma's suitcase sat at her feet.

"I'm Wanda, Wanda Wallace." The tall girl reached out a thin hand. "And you're May," she said for her. "You did it all wrong, you know." Wanda's dextrous fingers went in search of, and found, the new seams of her own fitted jacket. "Take it in just so, then they'll never spot. That bottled-blonde'll think it's her eyes playing tricks, not you."

"Takes an expert to know, Wanda," a girl who occupied the bed closest the window said. She was busy with a small comb on the head of the third girl who winced with each pull of teeth.

"That's Sue; she's a hairdresser. Thank God," said Wanda.

Sue waved with the comb before raking it firmly back through the head in front.

"Vera," said the owner.

"Sorry you're all stuck up here," said May.

"If your shoddy seamwork gets us killed, we won't know, will we?" Wanda lit a cigarette.

"I already know it's rotten," said May.

"A trained dressmaker knows good from bad."

"Tell her where you worked, Wanda. Go on," Sue said.

"Regent Street."

"Oh," sounded May, hoping it came close to impressed.

"We've you to thank for this view, I suppose," Wanda said, blowing fresh smoke against the pane. Vera coughed and was rewarded by a rap with the comb.

May lost them all at dinner. Somewhere along the dark underground corridor, which connected the main house to the mess hall, she found herself alone. Other girls made echoes of the passage and bumped fast against her shoulder, drawing in their breaths, surprised to find her there, occupying that invisible spot. Underfoot, the dust from old stone tiles changed the colour of her shoes. She emerged into the bright light of the mess hall blinking back the shadows and caught sight of Jan sitting alone, slurping back custard from a bowl.

"What's yours like?" Jan asked, not stopping.

"Alright. And you?" May said, sitting.

"Friendly enough but wish we were together."

"At least we can eat together, Jan."

"Only if you're quick, May." She pointed at her own bowl. "This was one of the last."

Later, after afternoon squad drill, she told the three girls she was going for a walk. They were free with their time then. Sue was fixing her hair in a mirror using the last of the afternoon light. Vera watched, cross-legged on the floor, while Wanda lay with long limbs stretched lazily in front, flicking through the pages of a magazine.

Outside, May headed right of the little pub, crossing into the road level with the tenement block. She looked back and up hoping to find her new home but the building buttressed before the room they shared, masking it to the street. It really was on the roof. She took a deep breath and a left turn into the unknown. In almost no time she found herself checking for street names, remembering the public order to remove them. She'd have to learn to remember her way back. She walked on, filling her head with homely curtain prints in a window, the chandelier hanging in the drawing room of a grand front room, big boots beside smaller ones on the front step of another, a gate painted bright yellow further on. Breadcrumbs back to the familiar.

May asked a newspaper seller the time. "Seven thirty, Miss."

Good, one hour more, then thirty minutes spare and back for curfew. A moment's panic caught her unaware when she tried to double back and found herself somewhere new. She took instruction from a woman in a cafe, buying a cup of tea into the bargain, depleting the cautious reserve of pennies given by Ma. May was hot when she eventually got back, chasing new memories like fresh ghosts, back through darkened streets that gave up nothing in return. Arriving in the nick of time, before the door was locked shut by the night officer.

The routine was easy to follow. Morning drill, then mess breakfast, followed by typing until lunch. The click-clacking of the typewriter board rapped without rest. May's fingers, invisible upon the hidden keys, joined the chorus and fired mistakes onto the white sheet in front. There, for all to see. Then afternoon drill to follow, marching up and down the inner-courtyard quadrangle, where if the girl in front was half a step behind, and the one in front of her another half, and then a third again, it sent a quiver down the line and the drill sergeant into a fit, like the war was lost right there. Night had its own shadows. Above the giggles, which came warm through the boards from the rooms below, blackout blinds encased their little turret in tomb-like night. She lay awake listening to Vera snore, until Sue threw a slipper at her and she groaned into silence. They opened the windows to combat the sweltering heat, causing the cheap material to catch in the breeze. Beyond, London beckoned with faintly audible cries, caught up on the current of night, until morning's rescue, when it all began again.

The first weekend brought with it a heat wave. Sue felt sick and stayed in bed all morning. Wanda slept through anything whilst Vera had disappeared before any of them, her bed made. May went in search of Jan, finding her eventually in the mess hall. Jan had a plate-full of powdered egg which she was mopping up with diamonds of toast. May bit back a grimace and slid onto the bench beside her.

"You don't have to wear that today, Jan."

"Don't you think I know that?" Jan said, tugging at the fabric. "Been on a secret mission early, I have."

"A mission? Doing what?" May asked.

"An errand then."

"Go and get changed and come with me." May made to rise.

"Why?"

"Secret mission."

The two headed off north on foot to the Notting Hill Gate and found a bus to take them up hill, through occupied streets of people and bric a' brac which spilled out onto the pavement. From their top deck position the streets looked lost below the wheels and the people, too. Eventually they widened, until the bus cut across a busy junction with an out-of-place Swiss house and exhausted its gears climbing up hill past grand, red brick mansions. Upstairs window blinds showed black still, those behind, waking to a different time to theirs. The two jumped off on the Hampstead high street and thought of home. They sensed the village knit beneath the city overcoat, pulling their own wool cardigans about them to make contact with it, too, to show they were of its making.

"Where we going?" asked Jan.

"You'll see."

They walked down a slim alley and from there, followed a broad hilly street up to a bushy opening in the trees, putting their backs into the steady climb. May led, focusing on the map in her head, imagined there by one of the other girls, Sheila something-or-other from class. They cut through rough shrub, pausing on wide heathland so Jan could catch her breath. London lay in the distance like a toy town and suddenly it was only a child's playtime war, until May caught sight of the grown-up blimps drifting above it. Down a dirt track they heard the sound of splashing. Angles slicing through water and the dunking of heads. Then they were upon it. Their feet thumping hollow on the wooden boards of the deck.

"Oh May, I haven't brought my costume."

"Borrowed one for you." May pulled out the red swimsuit, on loan from Wanda. Jan seemed to cower from the colour. May led the way, unzipping her dress, dropping it on top of the cardigan on the bench before kicking her shoes underneath and pulling on her own suit. Itchy hot wool Ma thought appropriate. Jan followed suit, scanning the bright caps that skimmed the surface one after the other.

"May, look, they're doing drill!"

"Attention!" May saluted before pushing off the board and down through the liquid with her heels. It took an age to surface and the water was much colder than the mill pond. She broke the top as a sky full of limbs came tumbling towards her. May sank like a battleship with the tidal wave and resurfaced to a spluttering Jan.

"It's cold," coughed Jan.

"Let's swim over there."

They made their way to a white ring floating twenty feet away. Jan clung to it and puffed hard. May felt the chain that anchored it there with her toes, slimy and cold, before pushing out. The centre of the pool was deserted and she stayed there, turning in formation on her back. It should have been busier. The city's lidos were closed, she'd heard, shut up and drained in case of a raid. A raid that might never come. They offered relief from the sweltering heat. Cooling jumpy limbs that ached with waiting, ready to take flight and dive at the first drop. Why the entire city wasn't here she didn't know, but she was glad for it. May swam over to the ladder and pulled herself up the rungs. Jan was already sitting on the dry grass beyond the decking.

"May, when we going to meet some soldiers?"

"Sailors, weren't it?" May teased, dropping down beside her.

"This chance might not come round again."

"If you go looking for trouble…"

"Alright, lay off," said Jan.

A whistle put them both on guard. The lifeguard was waving at the pool as though something terrible had come to rest there. Three women closest to the commotion swam rapidly towards the steep, unclimbable bank. May rose, looking at the unsettled water where from the froth, a man's head surfaced, followed by two tanned arms. The woman lifeguard gestured wildly at him to leave, standing back as he pulled himself over the final rung.

"I should whistle for an officer!" the lifeguard cried.

"You wouldn't do that," the man said, brushing the water from his limbs. "Besides, I'm good friends with most of 'em."

"Just clear off and find the men's pool."

"And where is that?" he asked.

The attendant, used to ruling softer bodies than his, lost ground and he moved past.

"You're very brave!" Jan said, up and alongside him.

May rushed to catch up, pulling her own dress over her head and catching the zip against the sodden material beneath.

"Yeah?" he pulled a cigarette from a pack in the shirt slung over his shoulder. "Want one?"

"Thanks." Jan appeared cooler out of the water than in it.

"What about you?" he said, holding the pack again for May. "Smoke?"

"No, thanks," she said.

Jan cut her a pained look but he didn't seem to mind. They stopped at the top of the gravel path to light them, him, flicking a silver lighter for Jan.

"I knew a man, a friend I mean, in the army with one of them!" Jan said.

"Yeah, what's his name?"

"Why? You in the army?" Jan asked.

"Navy."

"Us too!"

"Yeah?" He looked at May. "Let me guess, you're Admiral of the Fleet, and you're a submarine captain."

"We're Wrens," said Jan, turning the colour of her swimsuit.

"Come on, let's go," May said to cut through.

"Not yet," Jan said.

"So, you know our ranks." May looked him over. "What's yours? Petty officer, I'd say."

"Just an ordinary sailor, me." He smiled. "HMS Nairn." And there was something so honest about it, the way it caught up the freckles on his face, that she smiled back.

SEPTEMBER

"You're not a very good Writer, are you, Thomas?"

May looked at the floor. It was scrubbed to shine. Four months and still no letter from Ma. Jenkins lent over the desk and looked down at the list.

"Cooks, Stewards, Drivers, I've got enough of those to last two wars. Writers are ten a penny, too; everyone can type." She looked up, tapping painted nails on the desk top. "But where am I going to put you?"

The answer lay waiting somewhere between them. Jenkins took two envelopes out of the desk drawer. "Choose," she sighed, holding them out.

May looked at the punched-out print on both: *HMS Obstinance* and then *HMS Nairn* on the second.

"Nairn," she said.

It slid across the desk towards her. May took it up and read again.

"Today, Thomas, if it's no trouble."

Once out in the hall, May leant against the wall, savouring the something-new about to occur. She gave the dispatch over to the safety of her breast pocket.

Outside, May stopped the pushbike only a street away from the Wrenery. Keeping out of sight, she unbuttoned the jacket. It was impossible to cycle with it fastened tight inside such heat. The dispatch was safe still, held in the pocket by the little button that closed the gap. A last minute addition of Ma's. May cycled past the curtains and the chandelier hanging defiant in the front window. Much further on, the yellow gate lay pushed up against a brick wall and she turned her eyes from it, hearing children's laughter and feet scrambling over broken clay. In August they finally came. May got the girls into a train to pass buckets of sand up. Watchers on neighbouring rooftops sat night after night with their eyes on the sky. She had, too. Witness to the show of light that thrilled and alarmed.

She pedalled onwards, avoiding as best she could fragments of jarred metal and glass. Dispatch Rider was a thrilling prospect, too. As far as possible to get from delivering groceries for Watchet. Somewhere in thought, she took her eyes from the road and lurched to a stop, almost hitting a pram pushed out in front. The back of the bike jumped up, threatening to buck her up and onto the concrete. The mother cursed blue. Sophie wouldn't have. The woman carried on her way. Honor must be almost six now. Big enough to climb over rubble, May thought, hurrying onwards.

In the park, people spread on picnic blankets and the bandstand rang with song. A bus flew past her, taking the pedestrian track within to avoid bomb damage on the route. Its loud engine left a hole in the melody until it emerged again from the fumes, coughing its song over lovers and sandwiches.

It was another forty minutes at least before she reached the dockside. She left the bicycle against the side of a tin shed and looked up at HMS Nairn, seeing this massive ship made-for-war as best she could. She thought of the little floating tank back home. They'd painted *HMS Do-gooder* on its side. It sat at the back of *The Bull*, floating on oil drums. From the opposite bank they threw money into the hole in its tin roof, which Pa said did much good long after the armistice.

She took the dispatch from her top pocket and saw the ink: *CAPTAIN WRIGHT* penned bigger even than HMS Nairn, lost below it now. She looked up, as though this giant captain might appear to scale. Instead, there was one small body standing sentry on the gangplank.

"Permission to go aboard."

"How do I know you're not the enemy?"

May took a step backwards. The sailor smirked.

"I have a dispatch for Captain Wright." May held it out.

"No unauthorised persons allowed. Sorry, love."

"Leave her alone, Jim."

"You," May said, looking past him.

"One regular sailor at your service," he said, angling to bow. "Come with me."

She followed the second sailor up the gangplank.

"It's John."

"What is?"

"My name," he said. "Sorry if I scared you at the ponds."

"You didn't," May said. "Jan told me this was your ship." He looked surprised and she blushed, thinking now how forward it sounded, knowing it was curiosity that had made her choose. "Can you tell me where Captain Wright is?"

"I'll do better and take you."

May fastened her jacket. The deck was hard like floor but bobbed still in the swell of a passing craft. She grabbed the side.

"Careful." He laughed. "Is this your first time?"

"Course not."

"No?"

"HMS Do-gooder."

"Not heard of her."

"There are so many boats," she said, leaning against the side and looking across the dock.

"They'll be one less in a few months," he said, joining her.

"It must be nice to go away."

"It ain't a holiday, if that's what you mean."

"No, of course."

"Fancy the chances, hey?" he said. "Us meeting again, like fate."

"Is he up there?" She pointed at the forward level, barred by chain.

"Yes, I can't come any further."

"Thanks, then, I'll tell Jan I saw you, shall I?"

"If you like. Hey, where are you Wrens based these days?"

"Same place we always were."

"Look out for John McKenzie."

She nodded and climbed the steps.

The journey back was worse than the one there. It was a sweltering kind of heat. The kind that made you feel as though you'd rolled about in the embers before getting dressed in the glow. May pushed on in a dizzying slug, forcing pace, attempting to beat the closeness that hung thick in the air while the city melted at ninety degrees. Funny for that time of year; it made mad dogs of all of them. She met a hill and attacked it hard, in order to bask in the down. Descending, the river dropped from view, then reappeared to her left. To hell with the heat and to Petty Officer Are-you-Shaw. Dispatch Rider Thomas had a nice ring. It would be cooler still on a motorcycle, which she'd learn quick. Or, down by the river. May looked over. It was beautiful, the drunk September swell, where the waves glistened, even now, in the sun's dip.

She pulled over beside Tower Bridge, lifting the bicycle onto the pavement and down the flight of stairs at its side. Just for a minute. Just to catch her breath and be cool-breezed by the water's edge. Above, the traffic tore frantically across the river. Standing there, watching it come and go, she thought on what she'd tell Jan. How it might please her if he came calling. And at first, lost in this, she took the new whirring sound for the lifting mechanism, droning louder as it reached full tilt like once she'd seen before. But, it hadn't moved. The water darkened. A shadow blanketed its surface, sending choppy waves running against the brickwork. They soaked her feet and she moved back clumsily enough to fall heavy over the bicycle stuck upright in the gravel. A pedal scratched away the skin from her calf and she cried out, missing the echo, lost inside a sky of propellers. May focussed up; the orange against their bellies looked like pollen sacks. They droned steadily, carrying onwards, protected on all sides by smaller fighters like wasps that just kept coming. Like they were running away from something or had unbelievably lost their way and were embarrassed that they should meet like this.

Then the scream of the sirens came to meet her from above; it was the gathering spin of noise that threw the people into action. May started, picking herself up. She flew up the stairs with the bicycle.

Out on the street people stood and watched. The heat had sapped the urgency to run, to hide, to crawl into hotter spaces than this one. And still they came. A great caravan of noise. Perhaps they'd fly straight over and out the other side. Perhaps she'd clear it if she cycled fast. She climbed on, feeling hope fly at the first slow revolution. The bike was tired and she pushed hard to waken it. Something ran warm and ticklish down her leg where she'd fallen. An unfamiliar news agency building reared up alongside and then somewhere, the bullish dome of St Paul's in front, jumping left and then right, always there, impassable.

They spat up from the earth and exploded in the air, and not the other way around. The world turned upside down. Dust and debris rained down and she blinked its sting away. A smell came, like turned eggs and burning, like a foul stew boiled dry. The shattered back tyre pulled her backwards, like some demon hanging on the spokes. May threw the bike against the pavement and ran through the smoke, over grit and boulders, like a drained riverbed. Streaming tears burnt and blurred. It was the same burn that poured from the necks of the fire wardens, soaked to the skin by a change in the wind. God's life gift, raining back and boiling them alive. Over her shoulder, the distant sky was wrong to be so glorious, making morning of the night.

"Here! Here!"

She limped forwards and fell into a pair of outstretched arms, pulling her downwards, into night.

"Let us see about that leg."

The man passed her into another pair and went up again before she could wipe away the blur, seeing only the black

107

of his coat departing. She was guided through the darkness, singing out with fearful whimpers, and placed somewhere near the earth where she could feel. When the next roar came, she pushed herself back against the brickwork. It was a crypt. From her place, May watched the candles dance, threatening extinction, before springing into life once more.

"Don't worry, my dear. Are you hurt anywhere else?" A kind voice asked as it bandaged.

May shook her head and her whole body followed, unseen.

"Are you there?" The voice came again.

"Yes, sorry." Home was what she wanted. Another familiar voice. "What's that smell?"

"Winter jasmine in the alcoves. I used to grow it in our last parish."

"I don't know where I am."

"You're here and not up there."

The crypt door opened again and two dust-drenched people fell in. Those closest, rushed to hoist them the few inches needed to safety.

"He is out there now, looking to help those in need," spoke the same.

May rubbed the blur from her eyes which brought more stinging. "Who is?" she cried, confusing pain with sentiment.

"The Reverend, dear."

"Our vicar's wife back home used to call me dear."

"We are all dear in His eyes."

"It was just her way."

The sky ripped open and punched into the space, sucking the little light from the crypt. They were returned to choked night.

The smoke was acid. May crawled out into it on all fours. The ground, searing hot against cut knees, forced her up fast. By the cavity, the vicar lay on his front, his clothing ripped off, cuffed at the neck and wrists by a smattering of black and white.

Two weeks passed. Not enough time to heal the cuts to her knees, let alone the screams that flashed through her waking nightmares. After that first raid, which lasted until the day after, they all walked with a stoop in their gait, ducking at shadows, lest they be caught unawares again. That is, everyone except Wanda, who glided tall along the pavement like she'd had the nod from Hitler himself and a guarantee of safe passage through the war.

Since then, night after night, it caught many a person out, blasting them from bunker to kingdom-come. "God rest their souls in their holes!" sang Sue, out of earshot of anyone in charge, when fresh news came into the Wrenery of a loss to the neighbourhood. It was wrong to go about normally, but they did, and it helped. But not as much as the dancing. Glory nights at the Paramount where, once a week, they were thrown together for a couple of hours on the sprung floor.

It was Saturday and turning evening when they stepped off the bus for the short walk towards the Tottenham Court Road, their heels clacking meter-like against the pavement.

"Come on, Jen, keep up," Wanda said.

"I'm tryin'!"

"She's Jan."

"Oh right, yeah, course," Wanda said, slipping a cigarette into her mouth. "She's never come before, has she?"

"First time for everything," May said, looking back.

Behind them, Jan picked her way over sandbags.

"Look at her." Wanda gestured at Sue in front, walking arm-in-arm with Vera. "Slept like a baby all night while Adolf had his fun."

"She was lucky we weren't hit."

"I knew a girl found dead in her bed without a scratch on her, a right Sleeping Beauty."

"Heart attack?"

"Could call it that. Shockwave from a street away stopped the life right out of her."

"Long as it don't knock my hair out!" Sue called back.

May thought of the sign pitched above the hole; the one the bus had just missed: Unexploded. Danger.

"We should hurry, before it's dark," she said.

They reached the front of the queue and paid one shilling a-piece to the girl at the glass. Cigarette smoke and the damp heat of movement cloyed the good air. They shook their coats off and, taking them in hand, entered.

The sharp shriek of trumpet and call of string summoned them like an ode to forgetfulness, in whose ballad they willed amnesia against the dark world outside, to thrive brightly beneath the bulbs of the Paramount. Entering the fray, May pushed gently against waltzing couples, shy to enter what little dance space remained. She followed Wanda, Sue and Vera through the crowd, while Jan caught at her heels, stumbling repeatedly over steps quicker than hers.

Free of the mass, Wanda was first to a chair, taking a compact from her purse. The others stood self-consciously by.

"All right. I'll get the drinks," said Sue, disappearing back into the throng.

"Ladies room for me," said Wanda, rising.

May noticed the tables close by, where red-lipped women sat with men in their best suits. Frail and threadbare, some of them, and the lipstick cracked, like it had started life as something else. She pressed her own lips together. She could hear each pair laughing loudly over the band, showing to the rest what a time they were having, prolonging the leave given and the permission to play at what was before. Here she was playing, too, in her only good frock. The purple one. Mended and old fashioned. She dropped her coat onto the vacated chair and looked around.

"You look nice," she said to Jan, who looked startled to be told. "You too, Ve."

A waltz started up and the sprung boards were turned like a merry-go-round. Delirious-eyed girls spun past on the arms of service men, enjoying the dancing, their intentions still good as the night was young. The three girls looked on as the heads bobbed by, watching and waiting for Sue to appear fresh from the bar. The first drink was always a great help towards the floor.

Someone tapped May on the shoulder.

"Excuse me, Miss."

"John!"

"Are you following me?" he asked, the curl of a smile unavoidable.

"Other way round, more like!" said Jan, thumping him playfully in the stomach.

"Ouch!" he teased

"This is Vera," May added.

They conjured up a mutual hello.

He looked smart in his uniform, polished and pressed new like it was only brought out for now. What had he worn at the pool? she thought and then stopped, remembering.

"How did you know we'd be here?" May asked.

"This one." He smiled shyly, gesturing at Jan. "Wasn't hard to find out where you Wrens go to nest."

"Here we are, girls," said Sue, returning with a pair of dripping tumblers. Three more followed, in the grip of a grinning airman. "Where's Wanda?" Sue shot, handing them out.

"Where do you think?" May said, taking one. It tasted bitter.

"Oh sorry, there aren't enough."

"He can have mine," said Jan.

"I think I'd rather dance," said John, grabbing May's hand before she could protest, handing her glass over to Jan.

They squeezed in between the couples, effecting a fleeting nod to movement before the waltz cut out, leaving them exposed as newcomers on the floor. Soon enough, the orchestra started up again, punching at the air. Couples who knew rushed forward.

"Palais Glide's my favourite!" he said, taking her by the waist. They joined a rough semicircle of other dancers, linking arms down the line to face the band.

"I don't know the steps!" May shouted above the noise.

"It's easy. I'll show you." He moved her through them until she had it, crossing one leg like a plait across the other until their limbs joined the sliding pace set by the group. The tempo picked up and they laughed, criss-crossing and twisting with the smooth swell as it ran into a gallop. When the song ended they were breathless, leaving the floor with a new-found magnetism that had them bumping shoulders and limbs.

"My, who's this?" Wanda asked, looking him up and down.

"Wanda," she said, caught up in breaths, "this is John."

The next song began. "Do you jive, John?" Wanda asked.

It had a racy tempo, calling for movers with quick hands and feet. May suspected Wanda was one of them.

"I'll give it a try," he said, grinning and taking the offered hand.

The night wore on. May rested her step-weary feet on the chair in front. She had danced for hours, but not a second more with John.

"You shouldn't have let her take him like that," said Jan, sitting beside her.

"Oh Jan, no one took anyone."

"Well, I wanted to dance with him."

"Why didn't you ask him then?"

May was tired. It was hard to know what time it was. The orchestra played on vainly, the last song sticking to the next in a frenzy of sound and mischief, ruined by limbs grown increasingly reckless. Cries of "Get off!" and "I never agreed to that!" joined the boisterous blows, bouncing off smoke-drenched walls. It was starting to smell stale and unpromising.

"We're going on somewhere else," said Wanda, appearing alongside John like a wilted, week-old flower.

"Come with us, May," said John.

"It's a rather smart place," put in Wanda, looking at her.

"No, thanks. I've got an early start."

"We will," said Sue on the arm of the airman.

Wanda was off again to the bathroom.

"She insisted," he said to May, lifting their coats off the chair. They stood in silence. "She's a laugh, your friend Wanda!"

"Yes, we say that."

"I'll come by and visit you. I've the address."

"That's mine," she said, taking her coat from the bottom of the pile.

They left as a group, saying goodbye on Oxford Street. The couples disappeared into Soho, whilst Vera, Jan and May found their way to the stop, realising fast a bus would never come. The street was strewn with debris, with the contents and building rubble of at least three department stores brought down. They made it home in the early hours on foot. She sat on the bed and pulled off her shoes. Across the room, Wanda's bed stared brazenly back. May wriggled her toes painfully, regretting ever agreeing to dance one step.

OCTOBER

"Thomas, Thomas?"

"Yes, here."

May took the paper stack from the hand reaching out through the slit. She flicked through the dispatches, their addresses spread across the city, before stuffing them into the satchel at her hip. In the yard, there was drill going on. May walked the motorcycle backwards out of the shed and onto the street, forcing the stand. She yawned, sleep-starved. Since that night, the wave of heat had passed, but not the prickly, waking sweat that shadowed each siren. News of John also hung in the air still, made material by Wanda, going about like the bees' knees. May flung the bag across her shoulder, pulled her gloves tight and kicked off, feeling the newly discovered thrill which followed the first spit and grumble of acceleration.

That first spit. It was all she could think about. Tripping through her secret thoughts, racing her imagination into bends in the road she hadn't anticipated, and all because she'd got Dispatch. It was like working at delivery but more. It wasn't something Ma had begun, nor ended neither. Would Pa have thought her capable?

The post office had taken a direct hit. At lunchtime, May ate a sandwich from the seat of the motorbike and watched as soot-faced postmen emerged from the rubble with rescued bags. People still needed letters. To know what loved ones sent, what news from the line.

The sun had started its descent when she approached the docks. Since those days and nights of heavy bombardments, it was only a corner of its former self. More men scuttling

114

about than hiding places for them. She cut the engine and found a spot, putting a quiet boy from the mob that had gathered around the bike in charge and a shiny penny in his hand. HMS Nairn reared up like an acquaintance from a dream. John, however, was a reality, sticking to Wanda whenever they went dancing, always greeting May along with the others, insisting she dance their favourite each time, despite refusals.

"Boater Matthews?" May asked, reaching the tug beyond.

"That's me," said a figure on board, struggling to tie a rope which held the black canvas in place.

"A dispatch, from HQ."

The girl struggled with the rope she held, giving up to take the paper from May's outstretched hand. She was boyish with a scruffy, out-modish bob.

"Any good at knots?" the girl asked.

"I might be."

May took another puff of the cigarette and passed it back to the girl. It hadn't taken long to fix the rope. She looked out over the water where small crafts tugged slowly along with their cargo of men and supplies, destined for other vessels further upstream. From her low vantage point on the boat, it was possible to catch the flash of silvery-blond or auburn as it came loose from beneath the driver's hat, each vessel driven by a single Wren.

"Where'd you learn to tie like that?" asked the girl, passing the cigarette back.

"Broad beans back home," said May.

They looked at each other and laughed.

"Rene," said the girl, her hand rough.

"May."

"I'll walk you back to your bike," said Rene, standing and offering a ready hand to guide May up and back onto land.

After some searching around the dockyard, they eventually found the bike. May recognised the boy standing as lone sentry. They went over.

"Wow, what a blinding machine!" said Rene.

"Do you think?

"Wish I wasn't stuck tying ropes."

"Please, Miss, you promised."

They'd forgotten him.

"Come on, then," said May.

She dropped him into the seat and they took it in turns to wheel him about the yard, shooting at invisible targets when she flicked the lights on and off.

"That was nice of you," said Rene, after the boy had run off clutching his penny.

"Not really."

"Is there anyone special in your life?"

"No."

"A smasher like you?"

"It's getting dark," said May, securing the blue card over the front light.

"Come back whenever you like, May Thomas."

DECEMBER

"Are you going to miss it here?" asked Vera.

"Yes," said May, only feeling half that.

"She's lying." Wanda flipped onto her back. "As soon as she's out the door, she'll forget you."

"That's not true, Ve. I won't, promise."

May surveyed her belongings; eight months and the pile had grown. In the fading evening light, the empty case lay in the centre of the bed, surrounded by the shadow of things easily forgotten.

"I'd get lonely, a room all to myself," Wanda said, stretching out. "Lucky with John around, I don't have to worry."

"Here we go again," murmured Vera.

"Sorry, you say something?"

Wanda, she wouldn't miss.

"How thrilling, speeding around on that bike, important like," Vera said, ignoring her.

"I'll take you for a secret run in the morning, if there's time, Ve."

"You'll come back smelling as bad as she does." Wanda laughed. "Like an old boot!"

"Hey Wanda, he's here!" Sue's head appeared around the door.

"Who is, stupid?"

"Lover boy and stupid yourself."

Wanda leapt off the bed, cattish, and grabbed the mirror from Vera. "So long, bye, May," she said, patting her hair down. "Don't forget you're a girl, or the boys might."

Three months since that night at the Paramount and 'Wanda loves John' had become an emblem they'd all had to wear. "Stolen out from under you," Jan repeated time and again at mess, shaking her head, very Ma-like. The other girls hadn't been there, at the pond that first meeting. She was saved that at least. They seemed suited, John and Wanda, both with a kick in their step that suggested fortune followed. Something in John's smile when passing implied they were friends, though nothing like what Wanda and he shared. Faintly, too, thoughts of something long past came present, another bright smile that threatened getting in the way. There was too much to do right now, May thought, trying to forget. It was easy to put the bike between herself and the past, if she tried.

May lifted the case from the bed and took it downstairs, bound for the dispatch room and morning when she'd fly on the bike to her new lodgings: a single private room in a block in Pimlico with easy access along the river to HQ. The hall was dark inside the blackout and May used fingers to feel her way down the stairs. She was almost halfway when a shocked face came out of the pitch, almost sending her over.

"Out of my way!"

May dropped the suitcase which came open, the contents fled downwards, heavy items riding on a wave of vests and slips.

"I said move it!"

May gripped the handle tight. The face was so close she could smell the damp powder. Unmistakably Wanda's. She stepped aside and the spectre continued noisily upstairs until it was lost in the lights-out. She carried on down, wanting to be free of the darkness and to reach the lit hall below.

"What have you done?" May asked of the figure pacing the entrance hall.

John stopped and looked up, seeing the items of clothing which had gathered at the foot of the stairs. She hurried down the final few steps with the empty case, grabbing at the smaller pieces caught by the false light.

118

"You checking out too?" he said, handing her a scarf and stepping back.

"Is that what that was about?" May replied, reaching the bottom step.

"Girls, hey?"

"Don't forget, I'm one."

John looked at her for long enough to make her wish he hadn't.

"Couldn't give me a lift, could you?" he asked.

"You're crazy," May tried, in need of ground.

"That's what my pals say."

She looked over at the clock, "It's as good as curfew."

"Not yet, is it?"

"Oh, come on then."

May went past him, leading the way through the dispatch room door, where she left the suitcase beneath a bench. She unlocked the one to the courtyard. They walked across in silence, May, a slither of a second ahead, her heart racing further than that, and somewhere halfway, their fingers were quick to find their match. Their footsteps echoed lightly against the walls, a lulling togetherness that brought no change to the light slithers from the windows above. They reached the bikeshed and were lost to the complete night of it.

"Stop here," John said.

"What?"

"Stop the bike."

May pulled over, thinking she had gotten them lost. They were in Southwark or thereabouts, having crossed the river much earlier with the black-blue light up front as their only guide. It was the silliest thing she'd done so far. Wanda would kill her, May thought, still breathing shallow and feeling held tight by John who had stayed quiet the whole way, letting her lead.

The bike became lighter. She stayed on, ready to spin off if need be. He covered the flame of a match with his hands but she saw the tiny glow take between his fingers.

119

"Let me buy you a coffee," he said, coming close again, pointing at a building she thought was closed.

"It's late," she said.

"For the ride back."

May secured the bike and they walked over.

"Just because it looks late, don't mean it is," he said, pushing the door open onto the busy room.

"No, course not," May mumbled.

The blackout muddied time. Like not knowing which way was up or whether to walk back or forward. She sat down at the table John had chosen.

"What shall we have?" He looked at the menu. "I feel like celebrating."

"That's a bit mean; she looked very upset," May said, thinking of Wanda's bleary face.

"Not that, last meal on dry land."

"Tea, please."

"Tea for the lady," he asked the waitress with tired eyes. "Coffee for me and two of those buns over there."

They sat in silence, both unsure what came next. After some time he said, "You're the first girl I seen who looks good in trousers," and grinned.

"Surprised you seen any, carrying on as you do at the ponds and round the base," May said, cursing the crimson that hit her face.

"You won't believe me if I said that was a mix up," he said. "Wanda, too."

They looked about them, stuck for more, while the other tables rang with a familiarity they hadn't yet earned. The waitress returned with their drinks and sticky buns. Across the table they looked flat and the currants painted on. It still felt like a treat though. John took one bite and pushed the other plate her way.

"I'm celebrating too, really," she said, taking it and thinking of her new home.

"Then to us." He raised his cup and smiled.

It was a week before May had her first visitor and it came

wearing bell bottoms and a sailor's cap.

"It's proper nice, May," Rene said, eyeing the room.

"Stay for tea?" May asked, feeling the warm pot. "Sorry, it's yesterday's brew."

Rene placed herself on the edge of the one armchair and took out a cigarette. May gathered up the cups and gave them a good rinse in the dish water, looking about for the cloth to dry them.

"Excuse me." May said, reaching around behind Rene and giving it a tug to free it. "It's only been a week and I'm still getting used to it." She smiled.

"You should see my place," Rene said. "Cold down by the water. I don't have to stay there, of course, but I prefer it."

"In case you're needed?"

"Yes," she replied, taking one of the cups from May.

May dropped onto the bed end and blew on the lukewarm liquid, more from habit than need.

"Suspect you travel, too, like the other tugs?"

"Come if you like. I'm usually up and down as far as Tilbury sometimes. Have you been there?"

"I haven't been far," May said, sipping. "Just home and here."

"Where's home?"

"West. Sophie has, though."

"Another Wren?"

"My sister. She's not there anymore."

"And more than half the men neither, I bet?"

"Yes, they're gone too," May said, swallowing the liquid.

After Rene had left, May tidied up, putting away clothes and cleaning dishes. She worked industrially, feeling strangely close to Ma just then. In making this new friend, who knew nothing of home or the people there, she needed to confirm its existence. Once the room was cleaned and put right, May stood back to admire her work. It looked new again, like how the parlour did before a visit. She sighed, wondering if it mattered. Would any of it, without people to occupy it?

121

May drew the belt of her dressing gown tighter. It was a chill start. The kind that made your breath sharpen against the frost of it. She caught up the curtain and unhooked the black cloth. Like a lost cave, the room sparkled in the fresh new light, making precious relics of her hairbrush and tea things, left without care on the sideboard. But all hers. Nothing of Wanda, Sue or Vera. Everything had its place, wherever there was one. It was the first thing May did, to unpack what little she owned, remembering the moment the key caught at the lock, and pushing into the bedsit, big enough for all her hopes and dreams. It seemed so then, and with the spread of her belongings over the best part of it, did still.

Two weeks since John going, she thought, collecting up the cups, some lipstick marked, some not. They'd met often since that night. She placed them in the bowl by the door for the walk to the sink at the end of the hall. May reached back into her bag and pulled out the letters, dropping back upon the bed. She propped herself up against the pillows. The light from the window at her side played games with her toes stretched in front.

May read the address on the front of the first one.

May Thomas
Room 314, Portico Building
Pimlico
London

The thin blue paper folded sharply so that the postmarked side had on its reverse the start of the letter itself with the words, economically and carefully laboured into being.

Dear May,

I hope you are in good health? Don't be angry, I got your proper address from the boater who tugged us out. Rene, her name is. Funny how I'd visited and not known on paper where. Said she was an old friend of yours. She did give you up for a packet of cigarettes, though. I wouldn't. I enjoyed our first ride. Weren't those the best buns you've eaten! Do you remember?

I'd like to write to you if I can. You don't have to reply but it would be nice if you did. I'm no good at chat. Otherwise I'd have asked you to your face. Don't think I'm a coward. I'm not. I'm sorry I got off to a bad start with Wanda, it was you I was really keen on. I'll just come out and say it, May, I want you to be my girl. Say yes.

Yours, John
HMS Nairn, December 1940

P.S. If you accept, you will have to write after all.

She read the letter again, turning it inspection-like, as though just maybe, it might not say any of it. The paper was so frail, like it might spoil by being subjected to more reading. She took a sip of tea, cold, and stretched out on the sheets, tightening the gown belt around her. John's girl. The thought warmed where the tea hadn't. May looked around the room, untidy again but hers. Had this feeling been building for weeks, since her posting, or was it the fault of those new words?

"John's girl," she said, auditioning them out loud into the space. Nothing bad happened. Perhaps it would be good.

May opened the second envelope and extracted the paper. The letter read:

Hello May,

We got your letters. They all came at once because Harry Adson the postmans got a gouty leg and so we only got them at all because Mrs Adson bring them one day. She scolded him good and proper she said when she saw them all piled up at home. Had to walk round every door. Mind, said she got a few things borrowed back, so not a wasted morning.

123

We was excited to hear your news about being a dispatch rider. Are you sure they let you ride alone? Marge Wallace says Janet is typing for King and Country. Would not that be better, May?

We go on fine here. There ain't much to clean now there's fewer making mess. Pa took a knock up at the house. Do you know, they gone and turned the best rooms over to the army? What a mess their boots must make! Anyway, he's alright now.

Remember to stay out of trouble,
Ma

May gave another loud blast of the horn, thinking of the letters left on the dresser. One from John, asking her to commit some sense of herself to something written, and the other from Ma, bringing incomplete news of Pa she hadn't fully reported. In front of May, a van blocked the street on both sides, standing width-ways at a turned angle. What was wrong with Pa, anyway? she thought, wondering again how she might get past. It would be a squeeze, to run the bike up and onto the pavement. She kept the engine running and forced the horn again, as though it might move the vehicle clear.

A knock sounded violent. Did Pa hit something, or something, him? Were there raids back home? She must remember to ask when she wrote back.

In the rear of the van, a pair of makeshift curtains wafted in the breeze. Wasn't it an offence to leave a vehicle like that? May boiled, her mind running away where the wheels could not. What if Ma was wrong?

It was late morning, but the streets still had that new-day feel that came when most of the population breakfasted behind hot Anderson doors. The siren's long draw, vibrating against glass pane and garden bush, telling them to stay put, shelter, just a little longer had come this morning again.

She had to get through. The day wouldn't start unless she

did and a crowd of other vehicles gathered at her back, looking for a passing, too. Was Pa alright though, really? Ma had a Ma version of everything. Sailors were clean. Ma would like that, would take to John.

May struck out at the ground, doing impatience's work. Typing was not the same thing. The air smelt like burnt hair and she raised a gloved hand to mask the chemical smoulder. May switched off the engine and flicked the stand, raising a hand to the vehicles behind as if to say, "It'll be alright." She walked over to the rear of the van. The contents flickered into view, two perfectly made beds, no occupants. Hiding. Come out, it's over. She took hold of one door and closed it. Behind, a scorched torso from a dress shop sat propping up the side of the makeshift ambulance. Then nothing. No road. She went a step further and looked down into the concrete void and metal twists where something else lay broken. A pair of shapely trousers. But with shoes.

She backed off, returning to the bike. She turned it heavily and kicked off fast the way she had come, wanting to be far, looking for any place where it might be possible to feel normal again.

In the park, May stood on the bridge, breathing heavy, with the dispatch held over the water. The envelope smeared and disintegrated in places where she'd held it firm to the handle rubber on the ride over. Covered in red fingerprints now. It must have been on the door when she moved it. She wasn't bleeding. It wasn't her blood. May turned the dispatch in her hands. The envelope looked like all the others. Nothing marking it out, except the damage. What if though, inside, it held the command? The one that ordered the Big-Full-Stop. Pa was going to be okay and that was all that mattered though, wasn't it?

She leant over the bridge and let it drop.

NEW YEAR'S EVE

"Here, have mine." May slid the bowl across the table.

Jan dug a spoon in wholeheartedly. Around them, teacup noises kept up something of a melody along with chatter. May brushed the tearoom waitress away a second time and she buzzed over to a family, the promise of stuck pud already a lick around the children's lips.

"Wanda's mad with you."

"I didn't steal him, Jan."

"She's been saying otherwise." Jan cleaned the back of the spoon and pointed it. "Wow, that's nice."

"This?" May drew the chain up away from her neck.

"Is it from him?"

"It was a gift."

"You getting married, then?"

"And your ma didn't mention Pa taking a turn?" May said, tucking the silver swallow away.

"I said she didn't; why don't you just go home and see for yourself?" Jan asked.

"I can't."

"You could take that bike and, whoosh, imagine your ma's face!"

"Yours is pretty pleased."

"She's telling everyone I'm writing Churchill's letters."

"And I'm delivering them," May finished.

Jan smiled and pushed the unfinished pudding away. "Shame we don't see much of you these days."

"I'm always out," May said.

"And I'm stuck in," said Jan, blinking in lost thought behind the thick rims. "Sorry I can't join you and your pal Rene tonight. She seems nice." Jan leant forward. "Thing is,

May, I enjoy the work, I do. I know I'm just another girl at her board but when all's done, I'll feel I did something with the time. You will, too."

"Come round in the new year," May said, registering the false chord struck.

"When it's all over?" Jan said, like it wasn't a question at all.

"We'll stay up all night, like we used to."

"Oh crikey, I'm late," Jan jumped, buttoning her coat all wrong and gesturing at the waitress.

"I'll get it, Jan. Go, Winston's waiting."

"Thanks, May! See you soon then, like before?" Jan said, blowing a kiss from the room's end. May sat and watched as she was swallowed whole by the revolving door.

A waste of good fabric. That's what Ma would say if she ever saw. May stood before the mirror in the hall. Red silk, like a robin's breast and then, the silver bird, nested in her collarbone. It was warm against her throat. A kiss even. May tucked the necklace away and pulled on the jacket to her uniform. It smelt like petrol beneath the borrowed scent. In her purse, she took out the address Rene had scrawled on a cigarette card. The man in the act of getting on a gas mask. She flipped it over:

Gypsy Club, Soho – don't be late! R

It was a chill ride on the bus into town. She stretched the sleeves of the jacket further towards her fingertips, wishing Ma had sent gloves instead of the pencilled-down tart recipe. Maybe she thought she'd use boot polish instead of jam.

Off and into the street, the blackout was in full effect. On the narrow pavements May sidestepped couples arm-in-arm, finding the road each time. Old chewed-up newspapers blocked forgotten doorways and discarded crates made rat-runs of the alleys. In the darkness you could still make out the turned-off signs: Cats Club, Don's Revue Bar, Barbosa.

Signs which months before had danced jaggedly to awaken passing trade. Now, secret whispers rang out in their place, through long nights played out on the edge of glowing revelry.

An arm, light of touch, spun her round.

"Rene, don't do that." May raised a hand to her throat. "You scared the life out of me!"

"You're late." Rene leant in and kissed May's cheek. She smelt like damp tobacco. "In here." Rene led the way across the street towards a rotten door. Behind it, they pushed beyond a velvet curtain and down steps, steep to the basement.

"Take your coat, Miss?" asked a girl at the foot, popping out all over like a pin-up.

"I'll keep it," May said. Beneath, the silk moved freely, like it might slip to her ankles any moment.

It was brighter inside the basement club and she squinted to find a way past the tables, lit by women and men twinkling like far-off stars beyond the puffy smoke.

"Ah, sorry, May." Rene agitated.

"What, why?"

"I was told I'd get one near the band."

"This is perfect, Rene," May said taking the seat given. "This way we can hear each other speak."

"Alright then," Rene said, renewed and removing her coat to show a cut wool suit. "Miss, over here," she called. "Cocktails?"

The band, American, slipped through jazzy numbers May didn't know. Like a siren call, young lovers rushed like wind around the tiny space, twirling to a rhythm of their own making. The first drink ran deliciously cool down May's throat. She loosened her grip on the world above, like dropping back into the waters of the mill pond. Gradually, it occurred how maddening it was to wear the jacket here; to be the only one dressed to leave. She slipped it off and onto the chair and dreamed herself, willingly into the body there. May floated carefree through the liquid pace, tapping her heels until the waitress returned with potions new, to hold them in its spell a little longer.

At some point, the jacket must have slipped from the back of her chair and was returned there by a man at the next table. She made light work of gratitude, giving her full attention to the waitress, conspiring it seemed with Rene.

"I think I better not," May cut in.

"Go on, May, we might not be here tomorrow."

"I rather hope I'm not still here tomorrow!"

Rene looked pushed to the floor.

"I just mean, I'll have something new," May added quickly. "What about one of those?" She pointed at the drink on the table over. The man who'd saved her coat raised his glass and smiled, gap-toothed. The room seemed to slip.

"What's wrong with you?" Rene asked.

It was an ill feeling, to be ambushed by the past when focused forward.

"I can't believe it, May. How good to see you," he said, standing beside her. He was dressed in the greying blue of the air force, his jacket tightly belted to reveal a slim frame beneath and those eyes, searching hers for proof she recognised him too. May coughed into her hand and felt the little heat there, jump everywhere at once.

"Christopher, this is Rene," May spoke at last.

Rene was unmoved. There was an awkward moment when the waitress slipped in between them with the drinks.

"Why don't we join you?" he asked.

"We?"

"Yes, you remember Georgie, don't you?" Christopher pointed at the shadows.

"Make yourself at home," said Rene at last.

"Rene, he's an old friend from home," May whispered.

"Does John know about your old friend?"

"No more than I know about his."

Rene perked up when Georgie squeezed into the chair beside her. Christopher brought another over and placed it next to May. "Another round, please," he called.

"But we haven't finished these!" May insisted.

She looked down and realised that she had.

It was funny, Rene and Georgie howling with laughter like they were old pals, while they sat in silence.

"Do you remember when you won the fair?" he tried.

"I remember you making me win."

"Who told you that?" Christopher asked.

They looked at each other and laughed, or rather, May thought they both had.

"You'd win again tonight."

"We've both grown up since then," May said, serious.

"Quite." He blew smoke away and it went quivering, keeping time with the hand that held it.

May caught how it trembled and reached for something new. "Do you remember anything else?" she asked.

"Of course I do," he spoke quietly.

"What do you remember?" asked Georgie, slicing in.

Christopher took her hand from across the table. Her fingers glistened.

"Playing all sorts of tricks on May's father. What a beast I am!" he said.

May drew her own hands off the table, as though clutched unseen.

"Oooh, I love this one!" Georgie threw him off and pulled Rene to her feet. The two dived towards the pool of dancers. Georgie cried back, "Don't play tricks on his daughter, she's made such an effort."

"She's jealous," he said when they were clear.

"How's your mother?"

"Mother's fine, thank you. Look, we can talk, can't we, May?" Christopher pulled his chair closer. "I'm probably for it anyway, I'm going back tomorrow." Christopher laughed again. "This is sort of a farewell party."

May looked at him, knowing it would come now, the truth from his own lips.

"I took the money, May, that was meant for the hospital. You probably don't remember it went missing."

"I remember well."

"I knew it was wrong but I had to help." He swallowed.

"To help her."

"Sophie," May heard herself say, feeling it come out unpractised.

"Yes, I felt responsible."

"For Honor."

His gaze stiffened, but it didn't look like he'd heard right.

"What a great dancer your fiancée is!" Rene was beside him, red faced and breathing full. Behind her the song played on.

Georgie stood apart, twisting a diamond finger impatiently. "Christopher, I want to go now."

"Yes, of course," he said, rising.

"You won't see in the new year?" asked Rene.

"No," Christopher said.

"It was nice to see you, May."

She rose to meet him.

"I don't even know what you're doing here," he added.

"I'm getting married."

"Oh, congratulations then."

He kissed her cheek and it was nothing like before, as though the past was a dead thing and this last lie, all that was needed to prove it. May watched them leave, until there were too many in the way.

"What a stunner she is!" Rene said, sitting back down. "That John's pretty fast, ain't he?" Rene pulled on fresh tobacco. "He never told me you were getting hitched."

"Another drink?" May asked.

May stared at her face in the bathroom mirror, seeing the tiredness and dull; convinced it made up the sum part of her. She turned from the attendant to catch up a tear. There was another behind it and she slipped into a cubicle, where hidden, they fell freely. Sophie and Christopher. It really was true then. And behind that a deeper sadness brought on by their lies, and hers. May tore apart thinking of Pa. Like losing him all over again.

She emerged and ran the tap, splashing water onto her face. She felt cooler for it. It was going to be alright. Now she knew, really knew; it would be. The attendant took the towel when returned and they both held on, as the tiny bathroom shook.

May emerged behind the woman, watching her flee. Most had deserted, cutting a path up the stairs that were barely that now. The dust in the club had extinguished the light and those who stayed behind searched now in the darkness, trying to tear familiar cries from the rest.

"Took a direct hit above." Rene's face was close; pupils huge, like two spinning plates. Her suit had turned ashen and May felt strangely new and unharmed amongst such char. She coughed, trying to catch her breath, instead inhaling dust. A howl across the space made them both look up to watch as a man lifted something limp like a ragdoll from the mess.

"Let's get out of here," Rene said, digging her fingers into May's arm and pulling her up the stairway.

The street burned, cloaked in poisonous smoke they tried to hide from. They used the backs of their hands to mask it. It forced tears to May's eyes, calling back the ones she'd done crying earlier.

"Let's go back," May called at Rene in front.

"I'm not going down there to be buried alive, come on!" Rene held her hand, vice-like, and led the way. It seemed to May they went slowly, too much so, through the noxious fog, keeping clear of where it was hottest. May's red dress clung appallingly close, forcing her to wonder if she might die like this. Discovered as someone different to the person Ma or Pa might expect to find.

Like being pursued by every bad thing, rabid dog cries chased them along alleys and screaming metal came after, biting at the brickwork. Without sleep or rest it came. Then the ground drew in its breath and caught them up. She felt the pull of it, screaming siren-like for her to look. May covered her eyes, feeling them safer held. She stumbled, bloodying her nose and tearing her dress, to be raised again by Rene to scratch a path onwards.

They made it down to Trafalgar Square where the Admiral sat on his pillar, commanding from the helm like a madman in the sky. May wiped the blood away with the back of her hand. Past the lion on the left side, a squeeze of people gathered around the entrance to the underground system, many more than usual out celebrating, too. Some climbed his mane, spotting spaces in the crowd, shouting them out to loved ones below. Cursing any others that heard. Their cries carried across to where Rene and May stood. May looked at the other lion on the opposite side, to see what he would do. If he'd roar for his crippled mate. And he did, she thought, until looking up she watched as a path of friendly Spitfires ripped through the sky.

"It'll all be over soon."

"It won't, May. I'm going back to the docks," Rene spoke, decided.

"I should go too then."

"Come with me."

"I can't, HQ's right there." May pointed past the column to Admiralty Arch, beyond which there'd be a minute's rest. Rene looked at her and put her suit jacket around May's shoulders. "Put this on," she said pulling it tight," before jumping the stone wall in front.

Something of the madness followed May, too. Like now, standing before the night officer, barring entrance to the insides of HQ, like one for whom lists and doing right by these still counted.

"Where's your uniform?"

"Look, I'm not wearing it."

"Thomas, you say?"

"Yes." May pulled Rene's jacket tight.

"Get down!" she shouted as though a command, confusing it with the echo of an explosion overhead. May didn't wait, pushing past her and down the stone steps to the basement.

"It's crazy up there," said the first Wren.

"I heard, a right mess," the other chipped in, shaking out a starched white shirt.

May pushed the buttons through her borrowed one. It was quiet in the basement. Solid even, with thick walls for protection. She stood some way off from the two, aware of the adrenaline-shake in her fingers as she sent the buttons on their way. The three looked up together when something boomed on the street above, then they went back to ignoring her.

"Weren't you there when the news came in?" the taller of the two asked the other.

"Typed it up."

May looked down at her hands. The dirt didn't want to shift.

"Sad," said the tall one.

"Very," came the response.

So much soot mixed with something else. An oily mess.

"No one even wants to be a Writer, that's the unfairness of it."

May rubbed her palms against her new trouser sides, smearing off the worst.

"Probably all still sat at their typewriters."

And stopped.

May ran to be clear of them. Back above, up onto the street, Admiralty Arch looked on the brink of toppling, while the duty officer called over, urging her to come back inside, shouting she was needed, it wasn't safe. May backed off towards the park, until the voice became nothing.

Between the dark trees she ran, gravel sounding underfoot, slowed by the borrowed shoes that pinched, a half-size too small. She ran until her lungs hurt and had to stop, spitting sweet-tasting bile onto the grass, mixing earlier with now. Beyond the lake, where she thought the river should have been, the sky looked bruised. Rene could take care of herself. Another burst lit up the night. May passed huddled figures who knew how to make their shelters in the open, long before the raids made it commonplace.

Then out the other side there it was, the former Writing building, transformed into a mass of burning energy. Like the sun had fallen to earth and collapsed on that one spot, on Jan, licking at everything it could. She leant, some way off, head pressed to an iron railing, thinking she could hear the ping of individual typewriter ribbons shooting through the air.

When she woke it was light. May uncurled from the doorway, rubbing at her neck. The warmth of the blaze had lulled her, like a campfire at home. She turned and retched into a corner, breathing in the ash which hung thick in the air, remembering why it was she came to be there.

"No point looking, Miss, there's nothing left." The fireman poked through the heap, hunting tearaway sparks.

"Is there a list?" she choked.

"Over there." He waved towards a sooty woman.

"Thomas, where did you spring from?"

"Same place as you by the looks of it."

Officer Shaw raised an eyebrow but let it drop again.

"Did Janet Crawley work last night?" May asked.

"Friend of yours?" Shaw ran the stubby tip down the list.

"J Crawley," she turned the name towards her, underlining it with a thick thumb.

"Damned lucky, you weren't any good at typing."

"Jan was."

May didn't know how long she'd walked, or how she arrived, but there she was, staring up at the building. Hers. The route, blocked, had taken her far from her end point in places, exhausting what strength remained. The rubble seemed to scream, accompanying her like mourning cries lining the route homeward. Cries for Jan, May thought. Some of the noise and mess clung to the buildings which hadn't been hit, like hers now, caked in char. It got everywhere and into everything. She fought the grit in her shoes, rubbing painfully against fresh blisters.

On the stairs, she placed one foot in front of the other, to repeat. The feel of it echoed off the stone, oddly frightening. May concentrated on the sound of water yet to fall, to fill the small tub beneath the bed. Four buckets would do. Sitting in the shallow pool with legs crossed. No need for a small fire. No, definitely no fire.

On the corridor it was black like known night, the electric bulb burst and crunched underfoot. May put her hands out, feeling her way along the walls on both sides, past two enclaves on the left, in search of the third, hers. Where it should have been, her fingers found flesh, bone and bristle. She drew her hand away, surprised she hadn't screamed.

"May, is that you?"

"Pa?"

"It is you." The figure gathered her up, a successful shot in the dark.

"Come inside," she said.

"I didn't know you'd be here," he cried. "But had nowhere else."

It only took a crack of light to reveal it was the other.

"Uncle Richard!"

"Who else?"

"You best come in."

She drew the blind down and found matches for a gas lamp and candles.

"This all yours?" He dropped his case and walked over to the kitchenette, disturbing bowls and cups, steadying himself against the edge to turn back to face her.

"Got anything to drink?"

"I'll make tea."

"Been one hell of a night."

"Tea's all I got."

He raised his hands to imply he'd only asked, and found his way, stumbling, towards the chair. "I'll be back in a minute," she said, picking up the empty kettle.

Along the hall, May watched the water spurt messily from the tap into the kettle basin, relieved it was still on, hoping there'd be enough left over for later. Wishing later was now.

When she returned, he was asleep, snoring uninhibited, like one dreaming drunk. Uncle Richard spluttered, waking out of it when she let the kettle smash heavy against the single ring, her back turned. She heard him wriggle, creaking his weight against the chair, feeling him watching her from across the room in the quiet that followed. Ma never said he was coming.

"Got any fags? Someone smoked all mine," he asked.

"I don't smoke."

"Nor drink, hey. Thought you came here to have fun?"

"It ain't a holiday, Uncle."

"Back home neither." He rose and went over to the case, swinging it up and onto the bed. "Things have changed. Big House for one," he said throwing it open.

"The Park?"

"On account of the army moving in." He smiled, pulling out an untouched bottle of liquor that was concealed within a woman's dressing gown. "Lord Barker ain't himself," he said, handing the gown over.

"For me?"

"Try if it fits," he said, opening the bottle and taking a swig.

May did, feeling the slippery, fine feel of it creep up her arms. It was beautiful.

"Lucky he's got me. Sort of a right-hand-man I am."

May reached around for the belt but couldn't find it. Some of the flowers, she saw now, were muddy, as though someone had dragged them through dirt, and wasn't there a smell, like burnt soup?

"Where did you get this?" May whispered.

"Mustn't ask," he said, tapping his nose and sitting.

"I don't want it," May said, taking it off and giving it back.

"Please yourself."

The kettle whistled and May went back to the kitchenette. She hardly let it brew in the pot before she poured into two fresh cups.

"And Pa. How is he?" she asked, coming back over with them. The suitcase had been placed discreetly to one side of the chair Uncle Richard now occupied.

"How?" he asked, looking her full in the face.

"Ma wrote, said he's on the mend."

"That's not right, May, not right at all."

"He fall again?"

"Oh no, May."

"Then what?"

"He's dead."

It was the kettle whistling which told her he was still sitting there, sobbing, saying he was sorry. So sorry for it all. That it was him, come there, bringing her that sad news, that meant she'd never forgive him.

"It's not your fault," she heard herself say. "You weren't to know." Still he sobbed on. She turned away, not wanting it unburdened, cried off and given to her.

"She'll never forgive me, what have I done?" he said in repeat.

May went over, forced herself, and knelt to rest her hands on his. It helped the words to come. "Uncle, when did it happen?"

"Must be happened last week. Right one minute, then gone the next."

May thought on it. Then thought on all as it sank deep to reach the root of her.

"Jan's dead," she blurted out, feeling the tears come.

"She is," he confirmed. "It's just us now, May."

1941
JANUARY

Snow. Enough fall to make hundreds of sewn pockets for a new quilt, thick and with dip. It blanketed the land, the scene unrecognisable from the one she'd left months back. It wasn't altered by war's making as May prepared for on the bus journey back – why should it have escaped? – but by nature's hand. May raised a smile to greet it, to feel it crunch beneath her feet, recognising the stick-like footfall where the birds hopped gently through it, spotting in the frost-bitten sky the black of crows, like arrows pointing homewards that belonged only here. It frosted up the mill pond, the ducks under cover of shelter, or a few young ones, slipping bill-down and feather-up across the icy surface. May walked on, over the bridge beyond the front door of home. She opened the gate to the churchyard and left the cleared path to tread fresh-footed through the padding.

Ma's letter came in the days after Uncle Richard's visit and she read it slowly from the seat of the bike, not sure where she might want to go, knowing already what it said. Never got right again. May counted the stones lined up. Took to his bed for a week. The snow-covered names were hidden beneath the blanket. Weak heart in the end. May found it and brushed the covering away. Robert William Thomas. Pa. How still it was, as though the birds calling and creatures burrowing knew to stop, bowing their heads for sorrow's sake.

"Oh Pa," she let slip, crying at how sad it sounded. How cold her own heart felt. Colder than the frost beyond. Would the joy that was long ago never return? It was the memory of it, ambushing her dreams recently, which caused the most pain. The contrast between those pockets of remembered happiness – long summers thrown across his back, winter evenings leant against his knee and all the rainbow-coloured ecstasy in between – and now, where it existed only for as long as she could conjure it, in her own secret heart. She turned, hearing an owl call hollow from a nearby tree and wiped the last of the new tears away.

"Ma?"

May shut the door behind, clicking the iron against the catch. Voices, heard in the kitchen, stopped on hearing hers. The solid shuffle, that could mean only one person, brought Ma out into the hall.

"May, is that you?"

"It is, Ma."

"You coming in, then?"

May put her suitcase down and followed behind into the kitchen. A young girl of about six sat across the table. The girl raised her rag doll and waved its arm. May waved back.

"Honor, run and get your Ma now."

Honor.

"Sit down then, May," Ma told, placing a cup and saucer in front and pouring in from the pot. "It's a little cold I'm afraid."

May curled her fingers around it, feeling the heat.

"Half expected you to come on your bike."

"I'd never have made it Ma, not in this ice."

Ma looked older, and in some unfelt way, colder too, like she hadn't lit the fire in months.

"Did you get the money I sent?" May asked.

"It's up there, in the tin if you need it."

"I'll send regular now."

"His Lordship gone and given me the mill cottage for my lifetime. On account ob Bob, Robert, being such a good worker."

"I been to church, I seen him."

"We couldn't wait for you."

"May!"

140

She turned. Sophie was there when she did, the little girl moved, peeking out now from behind her skirts.

"Well, come give your sister a hug."

May went over and was pulled in.

"Don't you look smart?" Sophie said, putting her at arm's length again. "Ma, look at May's uniform; isn't it smart?"

"I heard you were carrying on in trousers," said Ma.

"This is Honor," said Sophie fresh, like it was the first time. "Honor, this is your Aunt May. This is the first time you've met, isn't it?"

May nodded. "I like your doll."

The girl wrinkled her little nose and ran over to her grandma.

"How long has it been?" Sophie asked.

"I don't know," May said.

They sat down. Sophie looked different. They were both of them older now than what they had been of course. Sophie, sixteen then. She must be twenty-two at a quick count. There were traces of that earlier girl here, more in Honor she thought than in the smoothed-down version of Sophie, who chattered on before her. She thought on when she had seen her last; at this table soon after the birth, and so different now, so something other. May couldn't pin it down, until she looked again and saw how Sophie's hair looked cut fresh, as though regular, and her nails, pristine red and free from work. May looked down at Honor on Ma's lap. Did she look like him? Like Christopher? The girl laughed, tickled by Ma, revealing a little gap between milk teeth.

"Where have you been all these years, Sophie?" May asked.

"Where?"

"Careful, May," Ma warned.

"Making a life, that's where."

"So Ma wrote to you too, about Pa?"

"Yes, he got to meet her."

"You said goodbye to him?"

"He was so happy. He said she looked like you."

May stood up. "I've got to go."

"Go?" Ma was next, putting the girl on the chair behind her. "Go where? It's thick outside."

"To bed," May said, thinking up a new direction. "Long journey."

"You know where your room is," Ma said.

Even here the blackout reached. May undressed in the darkness beside the open window, feeling the frost bite at her skin. Across the open field, something called, returning to its den. These sounds, she missed. She dressed quickly for bed and closed the latch, climbing between the sheets. It was freezing, the childhood eiderdown barely skimming the tops of her ankles. She curled up into a ball and pulled the cover into a hood about her head. Across the room, the magazine cover of the girl clung to the wall by its one remaining pin.

She rose before them, even Ma, and left a scrawl on the kitchen pad, saying not to worry, that she'd gone for a walk. May needed time for thinking, thinking away from them; the three women in her life. Now that Pa had gone, the house had changed in some unseen way, all traces of his presence swept into the grate. She needed to locate him again, and she wouldn't find him there.

Big House gate was stiff against frozen hinges, until pushing hard, it gave, unburdening itself of the beauty which lay beyond. The Serpentine was frozen up, its surface glistening now in the new-day sun. The grassy bank, crystallised by thousands of blades, ran into the distance like chandelier-glass. May blew into her hands and walked on, feeling closer to Pa with each step.

"What you doing here, Miss?"

A soldier. He must have come from the house further up. His accent was strange.

"I'm from here," May said, pointing back towards the mill to confirm.

"This is army territory now."

"Yes, I know but…"

"Did you used to work here?" he asked.

"Pa did, that is, my father. He died."

"The war's taken many of them."

May let him think that, deciding in the silence that followed, that in some way, it was true. A shot rang out from the direction of the courtyard and they both looked up. The unmistakable crunch of boots upon gravel followed. Marching.

"Go back," he ordered, also drawing back the way he'd come.

Shots, given at once and quick to fire again, chased May along the worn path home. They rang out, filling the sky with fleeing bird cries and the crash of falling glass that, in her mind, cut the vegetables in the greenhouses to shreds below. May understood what it was being broken up for – target practice. She ran, unable to see through tears and slipping on the frost in haste. They were easy targets, Pa's life work. One day, soon perhaps, those boys would have to do it for real.

DECEMBER

"Say thank you, Honor,"

The little girl whistled the words.

"I remember this." Sophie took the tin duck with its train of ducklings and walked them over the rug. Their heads bobbed. "Bit young for her, though."

"If I'd have known you were here," said May, not knowing what followed. A year almost, and some awkwardness remained since that last meeting, invisible still between them. Perhaps she had changed, and not Sophie? It was true, she had grown weary, used to a city of crumbling masonry and broken glass, that made her a stranger to this place of structure. Ma and Sophie still refused to say where Sophie stayed when she was away from the cottage, coordinating this next return for when May was home, too.

"She loves it, though," said Sophie, watching her daughter. Honor was off, on an expedition to the window sill with the rattling flock. "And this is for you." Sophie pushed a brown parcel into May's lap.

"I didn't get you anything."

"Open it," said Sophie.

It was light and soft. May pulled apart the paper and stopped.

"Well, something fancy for London, ain't it?"

May touched the soft pink leather of each glove, as though experiencing it for the first time. Had Christopher stolen them from his mother to give to Sophie?

"Don't seem right, celebrating another year," Ma said, coming in with a tray of tea things. "Move that paper."

Sophie swept the tinsel to one side. Ma left the tray and went away again.

"Why don't we stick a drop of this in?" said Sophie, already pouring the contents of a small brown bottle into the pot.

"Don't."

"It'll help her sleep."

May wrapped the paper around the gloves again. The sisters shut tight when Ma entered a second time.

"There," said Ma, placing a plate of biscuits down.

"I'll pour," said Sophie.

May was at the sink, trying to scrub the burnt remains of lunch from a dish. She heard the door behind her shut softly.

"They're asleep," Sophie said, drawing out a chair and sitting. "Why don't you just leave that?"

"Someone's got to do it."

Sophie lit a cigarette, "Bet you'll say no to one of these, too?" She held the pack out.

"Actually, thanks," May said, drying her hands and taking one. She leant across so Sophie could light it.

It was strong. She was light-headed on the first puff, taking a chair while it passed.

"Thank you for the gloves."

"Well, you're grown up, May."

"They look new."

"What did you expect?"

They exhaled to lose each other in the smoke.

"Bet you've got a sweetheart," said Sophie.

"I didn't go for that."

"Course not." Sophie bent her head, concentrating ripping card off the pack.

"There is someone, though." May pulled the silver bird up to show.

It was Sophie's turn to lean over.

"That's wonderful, May. Glad you're not lonely. Big sisters worry."

May caught something of what was before in the smile there.

"She can have my room," May said next.

145

"Who?"

"Honor."

"She's alright in with me."

"But when she gets bigger." May said, stumping hers out.

"We won't be here."

"But Ma, I thought, and it's safe here."

"Ma can look after herself, always has and so can I."

"Don't you want her to grow up near her family?"

"We'll visit."

"In case he comes back."

"Not that you know what you're talking about," Sophie said, coming awkward to standing. "This place would be better off if he never did!" She slammed the kitchen door. May sat still, with it ringing in her ears long after.

Honor thought it hilarious that the birds slipped across the frozen top of the mill pond.

"I used to swim in there," May said. Honor wrinkled her nose. "And when you're big enough, I'll teach you, too."

May's breath showed puffy in the frost while a tiny tug of steam came from Honor.

"Come on." May took her hand and the two slipped their way along the lane towards Market Place.

Once it felt like the centre of everything, but looking now, Market Place hadn't changed much, only shrunk in comparison to her memory of it. The cattle were absent, as was right in December, penned up in hay-hot stables on nearby farms. May fixed on a time to return; summer would be best, when they were out, and market day would be even better. It was important Honor learned. Had a sense of place, not got lost halfway up the drive of Big House and half in the dirt track. She pulled her jacket sleeves down over bare hands. The pink gloves weren't meant for her. She'd never wear them. May herded Honor onwards. The pair stopped outside the grocers. A poster pinned to the wall outside asked for more men. It must be ancient. May knew closed doors and garages were no longer forthcoming; it's what they all said. Somewhere like that only had a certain level of good stock, like market day, once sold and packed off, that was that. She held Honor's hand tight.

The bell chimed once upon opening and again when Watchet's door closed. Inside, May led Honor to the back. They stopped in front of the window of bright packets and jars.

"What you having, Honor?"

Honor pointed at a jar, its contents decidedly stuck.

"Quarter pound sherbet lemons, please," May asked, bringing out saved coupons.

"Just visiting, are you?" asked the woman she didn't know.

"Yes."

"Brought a little friend, have you?"

The woman attacked the decaying lump, freeing sweets which ran into the scale.

"Just under, alright?"

"And a bar of peppermint cream?" May finished. Sophie's favourite.

"You must be joking."

Outside, May pulled her coat tight. Honor sucked loudly on her first sweet, drawing in her cheeks when the sherbet hit.

Back at the mill, they kicked their boots against the back step to throw off the ice and powder. Honor, trying as May did, collected more fresh sludge than not. May lifted her onto a chair and took the little boots back outside to finish them off.

"Shall we go and find your mum?" she said, closing the door.

Honor jumped down and ran out into the hall towards the sitting room. May followed.

"Tea's brewing," said Ma at the knit, a pot in front.

"Where's Sophie?" May asked.

"Out."

Honor was all wool herself, bouncing into her grandma's open arms. May went over to the fire and put her palms above the heat.

"The room's getting cold," said Ma.

"Oh," May said, moving out of the way. She noticed the radio, on the mantle still.

"I was only telling Sophie," Ma looked over, "he was always so good to us."

"He was the best father."

"Not Pa, your uncle."

"Mine?" said Honor.

"May's and your ma's. You weren't here when he came last," Ma said, looking down at the little face. "We'd not seen him since the funeral."

"It was Uncle Richard told me about Pa," said May.

"Thought he might have, although don't know why he was there. Makes me worry, it does. He should be here, where it's safe."

May turned back to the radio. The needle had fainted to one side of the scale. It looked like it had given up.

May woke up. A thin slit of light showed beneath the frame, but it was the remembered creak of the board in the hall which did it, raising her up. She blinked, adjusting her eyes to the shadows. The moon looked high through the thin curtains, it must have been twelve or one, thereabouts. The handle of the bedroom door caught up and turned. She drew in her breath as Sophie entered and closed it behind.

"You awake?"

"Where have you been?" May asked.

"Never mind, move over." Sophie was already pushing her way into the tiny bed and May back against the chill wall. May lay quiet. Sophie was silent too, her elbow pressed on May's arm. May breathed shallow, her sister, absent for so long, now so close she could smell the familiar powder and sweat of her. And the alcohol. Sophie was dressed, playing with the bow from her blouse, knotting it around her fingers.

"Did you know the vicar's dead?"

"You been drinking," May said.

148

"Bombed out in London, he was. Susan told me."

"Is that who you've been with?"

"We been dancing, at the base."

"With Americans?"

"They gave us silks, can you believe it? I got you a pair."

"No, thanks."

"Suit yourself." Sophie rolled over to face May. "You know, if you weren't a proper little Miss you could have come with us."

"Hard to dance on your back."

Sophie jumped up, swaying in the moonlight. "When did you turn into Ma?"

"You said you'd wait, with the baby." May sat up, thinking of that earlier time. "You were gone when I came downstairs."

"And?"

"And I lied, to Pa."

Sophie sat down again beside her and reached an arm around to hold May tight, which made it impossible to say more.

"Sorry about Jan," she said.

The three were lined up on the bridge, first Ma, then Sophie and after her, Honor. May was out of line in front. They all turned as the bus rounded the corner and approached.

"If you give me your address I can write," May said, trying one last time.

"I told you, best you write to me here," said Sophie.

May knelt and kissed Honor. "You be good for your ma, then." She turned to Ma. "I'll write and send again, as I said."

"If you have got a young man," Ma began, "best you keep it. Buy a skirt. Boys don't like girls carrying on like husbands themselves."

"You coming or staying, Miss?" the driver said, wanting answering.

May was the last to leave, noticing the roadside empty.

She climbed up and found a seat. She watched them outside the window, waving. When she had left that first time, it had been just Ma. Now Sophie and Honor were a part of it, this idea of home. Pa hadn't come then, she remembered. He was up at the greenhouses, keeping busy. If only she hadn't gone to visit last time and seen the soldier and heard the sound of bullets being fired, she could have imagined he was there still. As the bus crossed the bridge and accelerated she turned to wave seeing more than just them. There was a large chain wrapped around Big House gate.

1942
JUNE

"It's rotten we didn't dock before your birthday."

"I won't blame the navy if you don't," May replied.

John pulled her over on the picnic blanket and kissed her.

"Glad you're still wearing that." He ran his finger beneath the chain. "Means you're my girl."

"Yeah, saw Wanda had something similar," she teased.

"Nothing like," he said, kissing her again.

"I got you something too." May pushed him off and went into her bag, throwing the brown paper parcel towards him. It was the one she'd kept since Christmas.

"A knife?" John said, unfolding the wrapping.

"It was Pa's."

"Wow, that's really special, May, thanks," he said, holding the small blade up so the light caught it.

She smiled. It was Ma who'd put it there, folded inside a woollen jumper, with a note.

Give this to your sweetheart.

That was all it said. She'd have to wait six months before that, she knew then. She thought about keeping it, but it made her sad, seeing it on the sideboard without a purpose. And why would she, anyway? She'd watched Pa cut thick shoots and rope for securing beans, why couldn't it cut through other netting? Like wherever it went, Pa went too.

"You can keep it on you always," May said.

"I shall, now come here." John grinned.

The next day, after seeing John again, which always felt

disorienting and like the first time, it was work as normal and late when May finally parked the bike and cut the engine beneath the block. The deflated back tyre almost held her on Millbank Bridge where it was slow going for the final hundred yards. She could change it and would, sooner rather than later. The heat made her nervous. Like the autumn before, when the sun had stewed the city and the people too, distracted when the bombs came and didn't stop coming for nine months. Nervous too, of the talk drip-fed from Europe, people being slaughtered in their thousands; women and children. She thought of Sophie and Honor, calling up every face as though it was theirs, placing the familiar on top of the unknown to give it weight. Closer to home, the nightly bombardment had slowed and they were able to breathe again, but for how long she wondered, removing the driving gloves and unbuttoning her jacket.

Up the stairs of the block and back inside her room, she changed into a light summer dress. Lemon with a scalloped edge. She smoothed her hair in front of the mirror, taking time, knowing Rene was usually late. She pushed down the frizzed front strands which always found a way out of the helmet to meet the wind head on. They'd planned an early supper at the corner cafe. Beside the door she picked up the heavy hand torch, its bulb shielded behind blue paper, just in case it took longer coming back.

"Why do I never get tired of this?" Rene speared another portion of fritter. The cafe was full, like the city had been hungry for months and was only now able to let out its belt.

"I'll wait for pudding," May said, pushing her own plate away.

"Bumped into John the other day." Rene wiped the last piece of meat around the plate. "Made sure to congratulate him."

"On what?"

"The wedding of course!"

"You didn't." May sank, thinking of earlier. He hadn't said.

"I expect to be invited." Rene grinned.

The waitress put two bowls down and left with the plates. May looked at hers, an overcooked piece of fruit swimming in a muddy puddle.

"Baked apple and chocolate pudding!" Rene said.

May sighed, cutting into hers. The apple fell over immediately, surrendering to the sauce.

"I'm just saying, a pal of mine's got the parts," John pleaded, caught in the hall. May barred the door, leaving him out in the corridor, feeling there was no good reason why she had, other than how unexpected it was, him turning up like that and twice in one day.

"I don't need help." May said, knowing she did.

"What you hiding in there?"

"Nothing," she admitted, standing aside.

"I'll bring the parts myself," John repeated, walking past her.

"I can fix it, John, I said I could already."

He made free with comfort in a chair and looked at her. "You can, can't you? You surprise me every time, May Thomas." He smiled, pulling her over. "That's one to tell the boys."

She unhooked his fingers.

"Come on, May, I'm going back tomorrow."

"Tomorrow?"

"Been brought forward."

She went over to the window and pushed on the sash until it gave, sliding upwards. The bike stood on the street below, slowly getting lost to night. She sighed. He hadn't come to fix it, not really. A small gust blew the pile of letters off the nightstand and she bent to pick them up.

"I won't be back for months, maybe a year," he said, coming close.

"Where?" May asked, picking up something of a conversation too.

"Careless talk," he said, putting a finger to his lips and pulling her up and onto the bed.

153

May looked at the pile on the floor. John's jacket thrown there, and her yellow dress pinned beneath.

"You'll have to marry me now," he teased, pulling her in tight beneath the covers.

"Says who?" she laughed.

"Your pal Rene, for one."

"You could marry her," May said to tease.

"I don't think she's the marrying type."

"Sounds wonderful."

"You don't mean that," he said, looking at her to see if she did.

"Would you like tea?" May asked, already up and going for her gown.

"No," he was quick to reply. "Get dressed, I'm starving."

They avoided the river, John insisting they take the alleys and avenues, saying he'd had enough of water for two lifetimes. It was glorious, tripping along hand-in-hand, bumping against each other at each discovered kerb – realising the absurd impossibility of both walking and embracing – saddened by the sacrifice of the latter for the former. Was this it? May thought. This gift of intimacy that would set her on a fresh path? It was new and untouched by anything else. It would be wrong to think of Christopher now or ever, and thinking this just then made her realise how far away that time seemed. Wasn't this a chance to forget guilt, inside of something new? It took less than an hour to reach the Charing Cross Road, lined with shops, news-theatres and late-night cafes. They joined the queue for the Strand Corner House.

"You'll look the part in one of those," John said as they waited, pointing across the street at a dress shop window. She looked up and saw the second-hand white gown hung there.

"Ouch!" he said, pretending to rub his ribs and pulling her close.

May buried her face in his jacket.

AUGUST

"Read it."

"It's private, ain't it?" said Rene, taking the letter and falling back onto the grass to reveal the tiny print to the sky. May watched. It made the paper translucent. Rene turned onto her front and read. May looked across the pond to the far bank where a mother was pulling up a young boy, soaked to the waist.

"I thought he'd asked you already?" Rene said, done.

"He wanted to do it again, alright."

"So why you showing me? Didn't you say yes then?"

"Yes." May took the letter back. "I mean I said that, but I haven't said it officially."

"Oh," Rene said.

"Perhaps I'm not the type."

"All girls get married." Rene lit a cigarette.

"Including you?" May tried.

"If I could. Maybe one day."

May folded the letter and slipped it back into her bag. It arrived a week ago, but was almost missed, hiding at the back of the box. Promises and vows were much to digest before breakfast, sounded out so official in clean masculine letters. On that first nervous read, May had to place it down on the bed beside her, should the words unbalance, falling off and onto the floor. She carried it now tucked inside her breast pocket, worrying away at her heart there, whilst she sped from one delivery to the next. She imagined strange things, like handing it over by mistake as dispatch, but whenever she checked, it was there, waiting. Her own private command.

"I'm wanted back," Rene said, gathering up the

wrappings and flask.

"Me too," said May. "I'll give you a lift."

At the bottom of the hill they got on. May started the engine.

"Least you'll have someone to look after you, when this is all over," called Rene above the groan.

"And until then?"

"Wonderful this," Rene shouted.

May accelerated, past people and trees, feeling the wind rush. It was, wasn't it.

SEPTEMBER

"Anything for me, Grace?" May leant against the dispatch window. Inside, the clerk flicked through the index. Headquarters held no secrets; here, everything echoed. The hall captured sound from all corners to bring them mingling, conversation-like, a second time round. This trick of the brickwork got May now and she leant in, unsure what Grace had said at first.

"There's something, but I can't give it to you here," Grace delivered again.

"So where?" May laughed, silly.

"Officer Shaw's office."

May took the stairs two at a time. She tapped on the glass. A familiar, nasal voice called out to enter.

"Take a seat, Thomas." Officer Shaw, clean and pressed new, sat behind a desk bigger than her. The last time they'd met was different.

"Janet Crawley, your friend, wasn't she?" said Shaw, remembering too.

"Yes," May said, sitting. "It was you told me."

"We've lost something else, Thomas."

May couldn't think.

"In the Atlantic." Shaw cleared her throat, unpleasant, and picked up the report that had sat quiet between them. "A ship, May. The Nairn."

"But it only just left."

"Two weeks does feel short, doesn't it?"

The room groaned, seeming to tilt, until May found sense to right it. "Why are you telling me this?"

Shaw looked embarrassed, pressed like she didn't know, until she stumbled upon the borrowed sentiment. "Always

157

better, coming from a friendly face."

Back out on the hall, the stairwell listed to one side. May fought back, steadying herself against the wall. Her legs, thick-drunk with the truth of it, fell to buckling against each step. She tried to fit the fragments together... Suspected torpedo, debris field, no survivors. John could swim, though. May knew this much and that was hope, wasn't it? At the pond he could swim. At the pond, where it was safe, and not both wide and unfathomable. The idea that he might have survived was quick to sink.

She sat down on the bottom step and searched her pocket for the letter. The date, penned at the top and barely legible, was already fading. Perhaps this disappearing would continue down, line-by-line, until there'd be nothing left but a blank sheet. She hadn't written back had she? She hadn't replied. What if he'd been waiting? But then, what if she had? There'd have been no ship to deliver it to, just an empty ocean and hers, one letter inside a mailbag of hundreds, sent to the bottom of the sea.

When May woke, it was late enough to confuse the twilight hours with the waking ones. She turned, restlessly remembering the hot siren-less night it had been. Outside the window, the stars were visible through the diamond panes. John had insisted on the thick black tape that cut coldly now across the glass like funeral bands. May felt for the pendant, holding it warm. She rose and pulled on her trousers, tucking the nightgown inside. With the rough jacket on top she went in search of, and found, the bike keys.

Down the hall and then stairs, where outside, she realised what a fool's thing it would be to have the engine roar and lights flare-bright when all were sleeping still. May tucked the keys out of sight and climbed onto the borrowed pushbike, pedalling it quietly away from its spot.

In half an hour she was in the park. May could see the shadowy mass of bird life drifting in the centre of the Serpentine – the whole flock together. Not another soul at this hour, only nature by night. May leant the bike against a bush. It became invisible in the shadows and soon her clothing too, draped over the handlebars. As she waded out into the lido pool, the mended nightdress drifted around her. The water was cold, numbing. She gave herself over to it, rushing in head-first to twist onto her back and head out, coaxing a direction with the gentle tip of her fingers through the flow. It was good, knowing what it felt like to float, drift as one lost. In the almost-dawn above, she willed the great sky to shoot its stars as freely as her own tears fell now. Another cried out close by, too, a duck from the flock, in sleep she thought, as there was no reply.

It was almost morning when she arrived back. She left the bike where she'd found it against the brick wall. She climbed the stairs and entered the room as one returning from a long journey, where everything is the same but changed. She shrugged off the damp uniform and nightdress, discarding them in a pile on the floor and pulled on the thin dressing gown, falling asleep as soon as it was tied.

It was late when a knock at the door woke her. May fixed on the person through the blur. "Think this is meant for you, Miss." The neighbour held out an envelope. "Got delivered to us by mistake."

"Thanks," she managed, closing the door and shuffling over to the window. What time was it? The street was busy, people leisurely going, instead of charging, as they did during the solitary morning rush. She turned the envelope over. The address curved at the Ts and Ls in a soft hand. Not John's. She ran a finger beneath the seal, surprised to see a birthday card with a daffodil-faced girl on front.

May,

This is late I know. I'm embarrassed to say it's probably a little young for you too but I saw it and just had to buy it. Take it as a card for all birthdays missed. I don't know

159

where to start now I'm here. I won't say where. You can write me at Ma's like I said you could. Do you know why I left, when Honor was a babe? When you went upstairs I knew it was goodbye. I had a plan already, you see. One I couldn't change. Not if I'd wanted Honor to have a better start, and me too.

It's so easy for some, ain't it? Do you remember how tired Pa always was, and he worked hard, didn't he? Some don't, May, but they get rewards all the same. I know you understand. I got help from one who could. I won't say who and so don't expect to find out. Ma don't know so don't ask. She won't say anything. She's happy for me. I don't want you thinking bad of me though. We was always so close, weren't we, May? I was glad to hear you won first prize that day. You was always good at the costumes.

Love, Sophie

1943
JUNE

"Why do you keep looking over?" Vera asked.

"No reason," May said, looking again as a group of girls surfaced close to the diving platform, the one she'd leapt from with Jan so many time to get to the bottom.

"You've ruined your hair." Sue pulled the comb through, yanking May's head back at a barber-shop angle. "Bomb go off, did it?"

"Shush," said Vera.

"Oh yeah." Sue stopped brushing. "We were sorry about Jan. We've not seen you properly to say before, but we were, really."

"That was ages ago," May said. "I'm sorry I've not been round. I've been busy."

"And John," Vera followed.

"How did you know?"

"Wanda."

This time, May brushed Sue away. "I'm going for a swim." She went over and climbed down into the water, floating out to reach the middle where it felt somehow private, somehow safe.

John had a sister, May found out. One who lived east. She made the journey over to Walthamstow one afternoon, meeting her in a cafe there. Marilyn her name was. Reaching past the teacups, Marilyn had squeezed May's hand, holding it, whenever she thought she might cry. The other diners had looked at them. The John she'd described was the same one May knew, only someone's sister and son. When it was time for May to go, she'd started up again, right there on the high street and May didn't know what to do, handing her a crumpled old hankie from the pocket of her trousers. Marilyn stood waving it as the tram pulled away, like it was her chance to say goodbye to him proper. May remembered watching dutifully from the back seat until they turned a corner.

May climbed up the ladder, letting the water run off. She caught one hand around a rung to squeeze the worst out of her hair. The deck above smelt like cigarettes.

"May, what a pleasant surprise."

"Wanda," said May, pulling herself over and upright. Wanda was head-to-toe in polka-dots, looking out from beneath the shade of a big black hat.

"It looks like the girls have played a trick on both of us," said Wanda, exhaling.

May looked back for Sue and Vera. They weren't where she'd left them.

"No hard feelings, hey?" Wanda extinguished the cigarette in a puddle near May's bare feet.

"I never had cause for any," May replied.

"No spectators on the deck," said the lifeguard. Wanda made to obey, but didn't. "You always did think you knew what was what."

"Wanda, leave it," May said, feeling underdressed for battle.

"Didn't count on him disappearing, though, I bet."

"Miss!"

The guard went ignored.

"Perhaps he went missing on purpose!" Wanda said, coming close and looking taller for it. "What's that?" she said, pointing at the little bird.

"What?" May raised a hand to her throat.

"He give you that?" Her colour rose. "What you give him in return?"

"More than you," May couldn't help. She winced, feeling the sharp tug as the chain took her hair with it. Wanda leant back as it flew through the air and sank in the chipped-out spray.

May pushed out hard. Wanda screamed and over she went, sideways into the green with a brilliant splash. The lifeguard climbed down and rushed over. May stood beside her on the edge, looking down, waiting. She jumped at the sound of the whistle, blown at the water, as though Wanda might rise to its tune. They scanned the tidy surface. Then at last, Wanda pushed up high, breaking through, a look of wild horror showing as she sunk red-tipped fingernails into thin air. In less than a breath, she was gone, the water returned to nothing.

"She can't swim!" shouted Vera, running down the deck.

The lifeguard sat to unlace her shoes at the same time that May dived in. She kicked downwards, feeling through the water as it got colder for anything that didn't belong there. She brushed against a motionless arm and then found another, heaving at the fabric to aid its ascent. Her lungs screamed for air as she struggled upwards with the weight, powerless to do more than kick and persist. They broke the surface together and Wanda jumped into life, punching out with clumsy limbs, winding May, making her slip below the surface, too. May forced her over to the steps where she was dragged upwards by Vera and Sue. May collapsed onto the deck behind her, breathless and in pain. A small crowd gathered around them.

"I never learnt," Wanda spluttered through a mouthful of hair.

"It don't matter," May managed.

On the walk back across the Heath, they all commented generously on how glamorous Wanda looked, her hair dried wild, which she seemed to relish more than the drama of her first dip. Wanda, in front, marched them onwards, dressed in something donated by each, a wool cardigan from Vera, shorts from Sue and a thick run of purple ribbon from May, purchased from a jumble on the journey there. Wanda wore it tied at her waist like a sash, chatting the whole way back, aligning her own recent brush with death as something earned for suffrage. May forgot the reason for buying it, perhaps in a way, this was it. When they reached Hampstead, they pushed inside a pub with a snug look, finding a table amidst stares and raised eyebrows. Sue made a beeline for the bar while they sat giggling beneath the winks and sideways smiles of gentlemen drinkers who would go home that evening and tell their wives nothing about it.

"Thanks, I suppose," said Wanda, smiling shyly at May.

"It was my fault."

"Three halves of mild and a port and lemon," said Sue, banging the drinks down in front of them. "What? It's for Wanda."

"We're to blame, really," said Vera, "for inviting you both and not telling."

"Unless you fancy a dip, too, let's leave it, hey?" Wanda said, raising her glass. "To the best three girls in town."

"Oh Ve, look at them fellas over there," said Sue. "Come on." She rose, grabbing Vera by the arm, "You don't mind, do you, girls?" May shook her head.

"I'm sorry I said those things, May, about John." Wanda lit a cigarette.

"It's okay."

"It's just awful he's gone and you won't be together."

"If he was here, we might not anyway." May took a sip of her drink.

"Weren't he serious?"

"Asked me to marry him."

"Oh May, I'm really sorry then."

It went quiet between them. Across the room, May watched Sue laughing, leaning on the arm of a young serviceman while Vera stood shyly by, his friend trying for the same effect with her.

"Can I ask you something?" Wanda blew smoke out from the corner of her mouth.

"Go ahead."

"Why might you not? Have married him?"

May took another sip. "Not sure I'm ready to belong to

someone."

"Oh, I am! If you don't, well, you're lost. Oh," she felt her head, "my hat!"

"It'll make a good nest," May said and they laughed.

May rode the bus home alone, leaving them waving at the stop, waiting for theirs. Was she lost? John had certainly claimed her attention, but what more had it been than that? She was surprised, when after the initial shock, she was able so easily to put him to the back of her mind. Astounded that it didn't trouble her more. That she'd filed it away in a neat little box, alongside all the other casualties of her own private war. Sometimes she woke in the night, sitting upright in bed, missing the bit of her she'd given over, imagining it lying at the bottom of the ocean, as well as the necklace that had sunk to the pond floor. She should be careful from now on, not to give too much else, or there'd be nothing left for when it mattered.

DECEMBER

May stood on the steps of HQ with the clipboard. Above, a small flock of birds crossed the Mall and were lost from view beyond the trees of St James's Park. She watched as a girl stepped up. She looked very young but then she hadn't been old when she'd joined, had she?

"Here for training?" May called over.

"Yes, Barbara Jefferies," the girl said, speeding her ascent.

May ticked her off the list and ushered her inside. There were five more expected. The rise in pay had been welcomed, five shillings to help Ma. Some of it passed on to Sophie and Honor now, Ma had let slip. Ma was a good conduit for the comings and goings of things. Things with real world value you could touch and exchange. It was almost unheard of, said Shaw, that position opening up and them needing a new Head Wren so soon. Couldn't share much about the one who'd vacated it, not much left. May had sat still, listening whilst Shaw stood at the window, eyes protruding from a face that was all flesh and cheek. She was the only person May knew grown fat on rations.

May called over another girl, wandering about on the opposite side of The Mall. The final four arrived together. They almost missed her. One girl, a redhead, led the others in a swarm once May had their attention. The redhead gave all four names after May had got them into line, letting her do that.

When the time came, May hadn't wanted to give up the hat for the other, despite it being a sort of three-cornered focus for each of them when they joined. Bets on for who, if any, got it first. Every girl started out wanting to be a Wren with a sailor's cap, and every Wren wanted the tricornered hat of the Heads and Officers. They said she was mad not to wear it but it sat clean and unspeckled on the high shelf in the room. It was the rider's one she enjoyed. Worn and flat. She'd sat on it once, an entire night at the picture house. She wore it today, the string pulled tight beneath her chin. That must have been what confused the new girls. Let them wonder.

"Not like that," May said.

They stood with a machine apiece on the white gravel. They held the bikes as she had at first, borrowed, like they were keeping watch for a fella. May's sat across the road, in front of HQ. They weren't far from safety, but in their new faces it looked miles. A truck of soldiers honked and called wolfish as they rattled past.

"Oh no!" One called Jane looked down at the bike newly met with gravel. The others abandoned her to silence.

May went over. "If it falls," she reached beneath the seat, "grab him here, and he'll be up and out of the dirt in no time."

They giggled.

"Officer Thomas?" A hand shot up and another bike wobbled.

"No hands, please." It went down in time.

"Did you get lots of, well, attention as a rider?" It was the redhead, Mary.

"Still do." She smiled. "That's not the best you can expect though."

They waited for her to go on, but wouldn't understand, not yet. Some, like Mary, might not ever.

"Drill," May said, pulling her gloves on.

"On a bike?" said Barbara.

"Why not," she said, smiling back.

"Sorry I'm late." Rene slumped low into the seat beside her.

"You missed the newsreel on purpose!" May whispered.

167

The film was already flicking away nicely. An outcast prince teamed up with a common thief turned good. There was a princess somewhere, too. It was the vivid colours made it exciting though. Like there was a whole kaleidoscope of seeing she'd never had access to. Moving blues, golds and reds worn on silken sashes and headdresses. This was May's second torn stub for the same picture. Maybe it'd get further along this time.

"Did you arrange it?" May whispered.

"Bloody freezing in here," Rene said.

"Honestly!" someone said behind.

"I am being honest!" Rene replied, sitting up.

They giggled.

"But did you?" May whispered.

"Yes. Thanks for this, May."

Here it came. The prince was about to kiss the princess, in a close-up which could mean nothing else, when they both quivered and vanished in the wake of a giant bang. The screen turned blue before collapsing to the floor. Those packed in at the front screamed.

"Bloody hell!" said Rene.

They rose and stumbled out, using the seat backs as guide. Around them, the auditorium was fast filling with dust and coughing. On the street, they breathed clean, cold air. They moved to the other side of the pavement, away from the mob who were gathered there now, seeking out loved ones unharmed. May looked up. The flats behind the Coronet had vanished. A tall fire blew in their place. The cinema stood alone, like a desert palace in a sea of shrapnel.

"Jesus," said Rene, blowing smoke from a new lit cigarette.

"I'm giving up on The Thief of Bagdad," May said.

They met at the top of Piccadilly that evening, beneath the boards snaking the buildings, reading Bile Beans, Bovril and Guinness.

"They should tell Jerry to clear off in big letters," Sue said once. "I'll tell them what to write!" They were only dark outlines now. It didn't matter what they said, only that the blackout made menaces of the people below, pinching and feeling for what wasn't theirs. It was a great relief when Rene appeared, finding May's shoulder above the glow of a single torch in a city of millions. They linked arms and stumbled off into more night, their torchlight dotting a path in muffled blue and red. They passed a group of people lifting a concussed man up from a lamppost base. May shuffled on, yawning. Bombardments, night after night, wreaked havoc with sleep and the waking hours too. When the days were short, it was harder still, throwing them into a dark age existence, squeezing their better beings into precious daylight hours. She worried for the dispatches the girls wouldn't have time to deliver, insisting they were sent in order of importance. Realising as the months progressed, and they came in thick and fast to match the speed of the advance, that they all were.

"Marlborough Place, St John's Wood." Rene brought the torch close to the address. "Told you I'd got it."

They looked up at the house, if it could be called that. A white mansion sitting back from a manicured front plot.

"Pretty smart, ain't it?" May said, thinking of the villas at The Mount back home. They were far from the mill and, on reflection, she'd never had cause to go there socially neither.

"I told you, Bridget's a riot!" Rene swung the gate and ran ahead to the door, rapping hard. It was pulled open by a breathless young woman, fresh from a jive in full swing. Its notes trailed after her.

"Do come in before you're arrested!"

May could have said the same for Bridget, whose dress fell criminally low at the front. She looked photographed, standing lithe in slippery grey silk.

"Irene!" Bridget's eyes flashed, knowing. "And you must be May," she said, kissing her on the mouth. "Aren't you ravishing!"

May stepped back, wishing she was inside her uniform

then. In the hall, a maid disappeared with their coats alarmingly fast. Bridget led the way down the corridor, towards the sound of high laughter and trumpet. May caught sight of her own dress in a hall mirror, feeling like she'd turned up for a party five years too late.

"Take this, and this." Bridget handed drinks from a passing tray.

"What a party!" said Rene.

"Thrilling, isn't it? I want you both to enjoy yourselves," said Bridget.

Bridget's hand went to Rene's back to move tenderly there. "Duke Ellington, do you remember, darling?"

Rene grinned like a drunk puppy.

"Won't be a tick," Bridget said, slipping off.

"This your secret life?" May said, swirling the ice cubes around the glass.

"What do you think?"

"Seems sweet on you, that's all." The tonic fizzed against her tongue.

"You think so?"

May nodded. The dancers cried protests as the record was stopped and something new introduced. A violin held a single note above their heads. May felt it suspended there and thought of the siren before it broke.

"Remember this?" Bridget grinned at Rene, returning to lead her into the cleared space.

May took Rene's glass as she went. It was just Bridget and Rene who manoeuvred through the slow and pointed stop-start of it. The melody was sharpened at the edges, forcing them to turn repeatedly, their hands held taut in front and their bodies so close, that when they strode as one towards May, they shared the mask of one new face between two. A circle of people watched them, the women blinded in evening gowns, falling to the floor in diaphanous swathes. The men were few but just as smart in evening suits and some of them, like Rene, weren't men at all. Applause like rapture caught up the end of the song and the couple stopped, Bridget suspended in a low swoon-like state

170

across Rene's arm. May feared for her dress. Perhaps the song hadn't ended? Another siren call rang out and she looked towards the illuminated action, waiting for them to pick it up. But then the all too familiar whine of it turned every head towards the blacked-out windows. The party was over. Coats were found and as she was buttoning hers, cries of "No Man's Land!", begun in a boisterous corner, spread infection-like across the room until they were all singing it, including Rene.

Bridget grabbed her hand, "The devil looks after his own, May!" she shouted, throwing open the front door and following the unruly mob out into the street, still holding tight.

"To mine!" shouted a man in front. May ducked, as did those around her when a loud explosion lit up the sky.

"We live!" shouted another.

Their laughter was terrifying. May struggled free from the grip and looked over at Rene, locked arm-tight on Bridget's other side.

"It's a game, May, to run from one party to the next," Rene said.

"You're mad!" she mouthed back as a shattering of rubble kicked at their heels.

May stopped, startled out of action while they filed past around her. Rene and Bridget had moved on, dancing close like before, while the party around them cried out the notes to the Argentine waltz.

CHRISTMAS DAY

May looked at the snow, pushing now against the window pane, decided as blizzard. In the park she'd almost been hit by an off-piste snowball, ducking in time. The boy who'd thrown it got clipped by the nanny and cried out at the sting. Frustrated woman, thrown out into the nether like him while the house was prepared. Ma's letter was tucked deep in her pocket. The scarf had finally arrived and she experienced the new itchy heat of protection in wool. Straight off, she recognised the pattern as the match of a jumper of Pa's, pushing it up to her nose. The letter, which was held between the folds, was freed when she unravelled the scarf and drifted to the floor.

Inside headquarters, the corridors ran hushed. Those on the daily slalom, doing the same back home, between dish and dining table. It gave a hollowed-out feel to May's walking not usually encountered, enjoying the company just then. Like her, there were a few other girls, but only those for whom no other place remained. That other place, obliterated from the land, found them all together in the mess hall, scratching out a path to joy through carrots, beetroot and parsley-laden mutton. They liked to see her there, although she was sure they wondered why they should. Imagining her country home as something safe and buttercup-ringed, unlike their pile of bricks, visible a short bus ride east.

Ma's letter lay now on the desk top, saved for today. To read it, would be like having the ear of Ma all morning while she chopped her way towards lunch. May got a fire going in the grate and sat beside it.

Mrs Margaret Thomas
Mill Cottage
The Mill
Fairford
Glos.

10th December

Hello May,

I got your letter saying you weren't joining us for Christmas. I sat down and thought about it a bit, but not for long as I got things to be getting on with that day. One of them things was preparing the bedrooms for Sophie and Honor. Sophie wrote to me and said she was coming back. She asked if you was and also Uncle Richard but I told her what I told you, I ain't seen him since Pa's funeral. I will write to her next and say you're not coming neither.

You know, May, I got eyes. Im your mother and I been looking out for you with them since you was a babe and didn't have the strength to use yours. I done the seeing for everyone. That's how comes I know you was your Pa's favourite. All that strength and love he had he passed to you. That's what you got now. I know you're alright. Nowadays, I been doing my seeing for Sophie. And there's Honor too. Don't you think she looks like him?

So you see, if you stay there, that's fine with us. We'll have a grand time. Lady Barker sent over a quarter of a goose. I been thinking on who got the rest but I ain't put the pieces together yet. Her boy's on leave, too, from the fighting. I not seen him but I heard he ain't smiling so much. I hope you like the scarf. You've probably got something more fancy but there you are.

Merry Christmas, May, make sure you eat something.

Ma

Christopher was back. And Sophie was going to be, too. That was good. Perhaps Sophie would stay this time. If Ma was on the lookout, she'd have a plan to keep her. Fighting didn't give many much cause to smile. If Christopher saw Honor in the village that might change things. And they'd be a little family. This was something to think about and May did, as well as she could.

"Dispatch for Officer Thomas," called a voice outside the door.

"Enter," May said, pocketing the letter.

"Blimey, May, anyone would think someone'd died!" Rene's face fell. "Christ, May, has someone died?"

"Rene, get in, I'm starved," said May back at the desk. She pulled the cloth away from the tray there to show two plates thinly laden.

"You weren't joking. Happy Christmas, May!" Rene said, coming over to greet her festive. She held out a flask.

"What's in there?" May let it hover between them.

"Just a little grog from the sailor's mess." Rene took a sip and shuddered. "Christ, my head; we were up all night."

"Gravy?"

"Rather not." Rene took the chair opposite.

May found two glasses and poured a slosh into each.

"To Jerry," Rene said bloodshot. "Let's hope he chokes on a chicken bone."

They drank. It was quick to work, clarifying and clouding in perfect opposition.

"How about we drink to peace?" May tried.

"Oh yeah, what's that?" said Rene, busy with a mouthful of cabbage.

The plates lay discarded against the wall. Slung after them, the tea towel soaked up gravy. They leant back, blowing smoke in contented puffs at each other across the desk.

"Thing is, May, I've seen an awful lot of her lately."

"She's very glamorous."

Rene took time to honour this. "Bridget says she'd give it all up."

"To be with you?"

"I know." Rene grinned.

"It's not easy, is it?" May said, thinking of Christopher. The drink was strong.

"It is when you're in love."

"That, I think, calls for a celebration." May reached into the desk drawer and pulled out a bottle.

"Where'd you get that?"

"Pinched it from Shaw."

"May Thomas!"

"She'll just think she drank it."

Long after Rene had left, blowing kisses down the hall as she stumbled, late to catch the bus to Bridget, May sat there. As the fire died, so too did the giddy feeling nurtured by the fizz and May had to concede, the first fug of a hangover was on the descent.

Rene finding Bridget like that was just brilliant. Happiness was theirs for the taking, but where the light shone so bright around her friend, how dark her own future seemed. When the war ended, what then? Would she return, and to what? Ma's errand girl, taking the long routes, running down Furzey Hill to try and stimulate the memory of the two-wheeled rush?

John had offered a way out. Perhaps if she'd have been more hopeful, it would have floated them both through the war and out the other side. But she hadn't loved him had she? Not really, not like Rene loved Bridget, as true as a meant smile.

She put her hand into her pocket and found the letter. Christopher didn't smile anymore, Ma had said. He'd made her laugh though, long before, hadn't he? Before Sophie, when was that? Everything past seemed far away and better left there. It was forward she needed to look now.

1945
MAY

"They named a whole day for you!"

"Shut up, Sue!" Vera replied.

They went back to swinging legs against the side of the fountain. May sat beside them. On her other side, two sailors climbed into the water, the cloth of their trousers rolled up to reveal thin limbs. They helped two girls in after, their own bell-bottoms turned thigh-high. One of them wore a sailor's hat and knot around her neck. Both men were without theirs, and so May couldn't say to whom the girl belonged. The four kicked at the water, laughing and having a great time there. May felt the splash of it against her back but when she looked, they hadn't even meant to get her attention.

VE Day. They all knew it was coming, for weeks the papers spoke of nothing else but wins in Europe and the whispers at headquarters said so, too, throwing them all into action as the reports came in louder, thicker and faster. Dispatches flew like crazy and she found herself back in the saddle like old times, riding high with a satchel stuffed with news, hell-bent on ending it all. Each typed letter hurried down the line, aided by ink reel and then petrol can, was sped around the city by an army of riders. These words, once read, becoming truth and truth, action. It was intoxicating. May was caught in a net of frenzy morning to night. Not knowing if she slept or ate, but never in want of either. Satisfied by a greater feeling, that word: victory. There weren't many she knew started with V and that made it special still. This manic merry-go-round, if it could be called that, sped faster. But it didn't make them sick. At

176

their work, they breathed steady, concentrating with heads down, but beneath, cries of "Faster! faster!" unified their secret thoughts.

It was only now, sitting quiet afterwards, watching the end unleash its pent-up power, did she feel the nausea come. The expectation of long-promised peace swimming in her gut. It was over. None of them knew what to do with that. For weeks her hands had been steady. They shook now with nothing to do and she forced them still beneath her, squashed flat against the stone seat, as though they might spell out the question on all their lips: what next?

The square screamed with people. Sensing it was best to stay away, the pigeons watched from the tops of buildings and from high on the column. This wasn't a day for pecking at crumbs. The crowd filled their own bellies with food eaten at street parties earlier on, moving drunkenly now as they burped their way to a decent spot.

"Not sure where Wanda's got to," said Sue.

"Not sure I care," said Vera through a stick of lipstick, applied wide-mouthed with a mirror.

"You waited all war to show some spirit!" Sue teased, cutting short the advances of a civilian.

"Guess everyone changes," May stuck in.

"I just prefer soldiers, that's all," Sue said.

"Here, take this." May handed her the little stick flag. "You staying here?"

"Where you going – it's mobbed," asked Sue.

"Refreshments," May said.

"Oh goody!" said Vera.

It was slow going, weaving through the crowd, held together sticky with bottled beer and relief. May bit her tongue by accident, dropping down onto the unseen level of the road, to be rescued by two pairs of outstretched arms.

"Have a drink, love."

"She has," smirked the other.

She brushed them off and looked back over her shoulder. The striped canvas skirt worn by the foot of Nelson's

Column, with its 'Victory over Germany' message was swamped by people. Sue and Vera were somewhere there. May wasn't sure she'd find them again, seeing how foolish it was to have separated. Remembering again how good the city was at eating people up. She would miss the King's speech, too, blasted out from loudspeakers. Two men had climbed a bus stop pole waiting for that to begin. She only had to walk back across Trafalgar Square to find Sue, Vera or both. They weren't really lost, she told herself to reassure. Not like so many others, making slow progress on foot across Europe. It was like God had shaken the world and they'd all tumbled out at the wrong places.

On The Mall, crowds lined the pavements, heading up towards the palace to celebrate with them. May had a job getting through to the entrance of HQ.

Once inside, the corridors looked evacuated, like the last dervish of war had blown through taking people and paper with it, leaving a trail of the latter spread across the floor.

Shaw stood inside the temporary writing room, surrounded on all sides by typewriters that jutted out in mid-key, abandoned at the last letter.

"Thomas," she pulled down on her jacket, "Officer, I mean. Sorry, I forget."

"It's alright," May said, stepping in.

Shaw moved down the line of desks, pushing the chairs beneath.

"Everyone's celebrating," May said.

"I know," Shaw replied, ripping a piece of paper out of a machine. "This address is wrong," she read.

"Don't matter, does it?" May laughed.

"Not to you."

"Come back with me to the square."

"What?" Shaw pulled out another sheet. "Can't," and then the next, "too much to do here."

May left her there and made her way upstairs, feeling the shadow follow as she climbed, the one she knew existed since peace was declared. It had found Shaw. She hurried, laughing to banish it, with thoughts of Sue and Vera waiting thirsty for her return. There were some remembered bottles in the cupboard of her office. May opened the door and stopped cold, as though the shadow had found its way to her after all and had run ahead, its ghost standing before her.

"John."

"Hello May."

His cap sat upon the desk beside him. He had moved the lamp over to be able to lean there, and somehow that action, the movement of something outside him, made him seem more real by its misplacement. John rose and walked halfway towards her, stopping until she moved too, and May, aware it was something he expected, did too. In the silence, he reached his hands around her face and kissed her.

"You look worse than me!" he joked. It was one he seemed unsure of making.

"Kiss me again?" she asked, wanting a moment hidden.

He did, and afterwards she remembered the beer. Going to the cupboard for the bottles there.

"Here," he said, taking both and breaking the tops off against the desk. May took one. They tapped the stems together and poured the liquid back. It was warm and unpleasant. How long ago had she put it there? Before he went missing.

"When did you get back?" she asked, pulling out a chair.

"A week ago, I think," he said, pulling across the other. "They had me in debriefing."

"Are you hungry?"

"I know," he said, making a show of how big his clothes were. "They don't feed you too good in camp."

"Where?"

"Milag Nord, Bremen."

It sounded harsh and uncaring. He lit a cigarette and offered her one. She shook her head.

"Germans picked up the lifeboat." He strained against the tip. "We didn't all make it back to land."

"I saw your sister."

"I'm going there next."

179

Thoughts of home brushed the shadows from his face for a moment and they smiled politely. May handed him another two bottles.

"Did you get my letter?" he asked.

"I tried to reply," she said, unsure of what she meant.

She asked for a cigarette then, him reaching out to light it with a match.

"The war stopped many things," he said, rising and going to the window.

"I should have known it; a bloke!" Wanda stood at the door in vivid red, white and blue; a patriotic doll. "My God, John. You're not dead." She blanched.

"Hello Wanda." His grin was all at once one May remembered. "You look smashing!"

"What, this?" Wanda's colour rose to match one of the stripes. "You must remember."

"Do you want a beer, Wanda?" May asked, meaning to find her one.

"Oh God, I'm sorry," Wanda said of the moment. "I'll leave you two. Ve and Sue's outside." She raised a hand and was gone.

"She ain't changed," he said.

May didn't much feel like returning to the celebrations after he'd left. The beer made her dizzy but they'd parted soberly, with all the formalities of love remembered. She couldn't explain away her crossness, irked by an irrationality clouded by drink. His showing up left a hole in her memory, forcing her to chuck out the loving idea of him for this new one. It wasn't his fault, although his being there demanded that she call up the memory of her former self, too. As though he expected it. She wasn't sure she could. Or wanted to. He was safe and come home. She was thankful, God, was she for that. Marilyn would faint clean away. May looked out of the window. All of London embraced there, while she watched through the glass. Then grew the rising realisation she was being watched.

"Someone's trying to get you on the switchboard," Shaw

said, holding up the entrance with a thick arm.

"Can you put it through here?"

"Yes, Ma'am," she said, finding fun in the reply.

Six minutes before the phone rang. The line crackled as Shaw punched it through.

"Christ's sake, May, where you been?"

It was Sophie. Far away.

"What's wrong? Is it Honor?" May's insides went cartwheeling.

"No, not Honor; she's here now."

The phone was dropped.

"Ello Aunty May."

"Hello Honor." She wanted Sophie. Something in her voice.

"I'm sleeping in your room."

"Put your Ma on, Honor."

May held the receiver away while it was scratched up Sophie's coat.

"Ma's been taken ill," Sophie told.

"With what?"

"The doctors found me and I came this morning."

"Sophie."

"Because I'm oldest."

"What it is?"

"She's had a stroke."

"A stroke?"

"She ain't moving and she ain't talking but she ain't dead."

"I'm coming home."

"I think you better."

The line clicked off.

PART THREE

1945
JUNE

The bus pulled up hard outside the village. May jumped off with the other passengers, a group of refugees from the city, while the driver sent a boy ahead to Norton's Yard for an answer to the fizzing engine. May wondered if he would return with a steamer as tow. What if it'd been sold for plane parts? She looked at the other passengers piled off now, some shunting up the grass bank atop beaten suitcases while those able, made a slow march of the final mile. They made an odd caravan, dressed in regular civilian clothes, like they hadn't given much thought to fashion for years. May retrieved her case from the pile and joined the mismatched train. The case hit regular like the tick of a clock against her leg. It was stuffed full. Despite this, May thought about what got left behind, everyday things like a pot, a pan and the teacups with technicolour cottages painted on dainty bellies. Paraphernalia of an independent existence. The leaving of which still weighed heavy on her mind.

When the time came to go, she'd first stuffed the satchel full of letters, almost instinctively, knowing that's where dispatch went. Although it was a hollow gesture because the urgency to deliver had left. The last letter she'd received was postmarked Walthamstow and dated a week ago, and that she hadn't opened. In fact, since Sophie ringing, May had been the one to write home, and she did so, solidly for weeks while waiting to be discharged. Knowing that to leave in a rush would have made no difference. There weren't any seats on the buses for weeks. It seemed the end brought with it an immediate plunge back into domesticity.

185

The fighting was hummed about, whistled in tunes on the street where you got tapped on the shoulder, "Hey, what did you do?"

"Dispatch."

"My wife too, you know her?" She never did. May saw in the eyes of the other girls, dreams of marriage cooked up in place of victory, as though the two carried equal weight.

Despite the unopened letter, she hadn't seen John yet, missing him when he came by the flat and getting halfway to Walthamstow herself before turning back.

"It's crazy, isn't it?" he said on the line before she left. She had to agree it was. Then there was what lay ahead.

The country road melted slippery in the midday heat. Each time a motorcar passed, May found herself eyeing the driver, to see if it was Christopher because, the closer she got to this place, to this sense of home, the stronger the remembrances came. Stupid, really. He said he'd sold it years before and never smiled anyway.

These things palled into nothingness though when she thought of Ma. May was embarrassed to find her changed as Sophie said she was, writing to say she had regained the tiny movement in her fingers and eyelids but still hadn't spoken. When it was Ma did all the talking, how could May compensate them both?

"Hello?"

May's call went unanswered. She closed the door of the mill cottage gentle, it sounded in turn, clicking loudly on the catch for want of anything better to fill the space. The house was in shadows, like it had its eyes shut against homecomings. May poked into the kitchen, confirming what she thought was true. They were out. Visiting Ma, still at the cottage hospital. She'd unpack and go too. May climbed the stairs, thinking it felt like stealing in, as though her time for doing so had passed. On the first landing, Ma's door showed a crack. Enough for a tiny gasp to steal out into the space and greet May as she passed. May leant in and pushed the panel so the door opened, revealing what

186

could be Ma, lost beneath the blankets. Was she here alone?

She left the case in the hall and went in and over to the bed. Ma's face was just visible, poking out from inside the bizarre pile of cloth, like everything they owned had been placed right there. The face was rendered concrete, absolute in its stillness. Ma was like a waxen version of her living self, the skin a single shade, not moved to colour in one area over another. All still, all except the eyes, which danced powerful, firing meaning for the mouth and hands. May found their colour changed, blackened in the metamorphosis from animation to thought. Ma had never been one to reflect long on anything, May recalled, and now thought was the only tool she had to chisel away at the world, through glances, blinks and stares.

"I'm back, Ma."

The eyes looked still to the wall.

"Where's Sophie?" May asked sitting, checking herself against future questions.

She lifted the covers and found Ma's hand, laying hers on top, cocooning it there. It was warm. The room was bright, almost cheerful in hue, absorbing the light through threadbare curtains that long ago had lost their meaning. Freed breath, from inside Ma, tumbled limply from her lips. May squeezed her hand and looked into the black blankness to see if she could find its meaning there. She heard this first conversation fought between them, playing both parts badly. May sighed, looking back at the door and caught sight of the corner of her case in the hall.

No sooner had the kitchen door slammed, footsteps came on the stairs; Sophie. It was Honor burst into the room first. She was grown tall, unlike her mother, with none of her lightness, her eyes heavy set and shaded beneath so she looked sad even when smiling. She stopped in the frame, looking shyly at May before opening her mouth to speak. The gap between her teeth had closed.

"I thought I could smell engine oil!" Sophie stood behind her smiling, her hands on Honor's shoulders. "Run and give Grandma her flowers."

Honor walked towards the bed with the daisies clutched. "Aunt May." She reached over and pecked hen-like at May's cheek. "These for you, Grandma," she said, holding them to Ma's face. They looked half-expired. Ma's eyes animated. Honor seemed to register the change, scrunching up her nose. "I think she said thank you," she said, looking back at Sophie.

"She did, Honor. Now go downstairs and find a vase."

Sophie moved aside and waited until she heard her moving in the cupboards far below, before going over to the place beside May.

"You look good, May," she said, first embracing and then holding her at arm's length to check she meant it.

"How is she?" May asked.

"Not here." Sophie smiled. She turned to Ma, "Isn't it good May's home, Ma?"

May sensed some change as this time the eyes brushed hers. They had understood each other. May was relieved somehow that nothing had changed.

"Everything's changed," said Sophie unbuttoning her cardigan, "You'll find there's less men around. Mrs Layton from the concession lost both her boys, right at the end too, so sad. She's stopped selling their favourite sweets, tragic, mine, too."

"You coping?" May asked.

"I wrote, didn't I?" Sophie rose. "You're not the only one can do things. You ain't brought up a child."

"Just tell me where to pitch in," May said.

Sophie stood at the curtains, opened now. "Let's go and make tea," she said, the day lighting upon her made-up face.

It felt wrong to leave Ma there. On her third attempt, May found the cups. Sophie had moved them to a different spot. May placed them unheard on the table, feeling that Ma might take offence at the sound of movement below, like they had no right to go about any of it with her above.

"Life don't stop, May," Sophie said, throwing drawers open in search of spoons and clashing pots out of the way on the hunt for the biscuit jar.

"Didn't it live up there?" May said, pointing at the dresser top.

"When we were five perhaps," came the reply.

She was sure it had last time she came. The daisies recuperated in a vase on the table, their stalks grown fat on water. May looked over at Honor, sitting across from her. Where was Christopher now? She couldn't find the likeness, like all the years of not speaking about him had erased him altogether from her make-up.

"You've grown tall, Honor," May said instead.

"She ain't like none of us, that's true," said Sophie, pouring from the pot.

"Height was more Pa's side," May said, munching on a biscuit. The jar had turned up beneath the sink.

"Ma says she stretched me at birth," said Honor, reaching for a biscuit.

"It's true," said Sophie, sipping loudly from her own steaming cup. "Actually, it'd be good, May, if you could sort the plot."

"Pa's?"

"We don't know how." Mother and daughter looked at each other. May remembered when they'd shared looks like that.

"I'll have a go," she said, raking the biscuit crumbs on the table into a little pile.

JULY

"I need it sharpening," May said, standing outside the engine house on The Crofts. Herbert Briggs took up the spade and looked at the edge.

"Gone rusty, too. I've got something that'll sort that." He went back inside the workshop. "Follow me."

She went into the gloom. It took her eyes a while to adjust but it was welcome relief from the sun's glare. May followed him to the back of the workshop, past the agricultural machines, glad they were intact, like heroes of her childhood memories. The engine master knelt to his task, running a dirty cloth along the tip of the spade. He dipped it back in the jar, bringing out more grease.

"You don't half look like your Pa," he said, looking up.

"I can't get the spade in as deep as him."

"Takes practice." He smiled.

"Is this the Fowler?" She reached out, running her hand up one of the giant wheel spokes at her side.

"It is that."

"I remember it winning first prize."

"As did you, I recall," he said. "You know, that was the last carnival year."

"It might return," she replied.

"But so many haven't." He held the blade up and, satisfied, returned to rubbing at the other side. "You women doing alright over there?"

"Course." She wiped the grease from the spoke on her trouser side. "Shall I come back for it later?"

"As you like."

Out in the sun, May squinted. Sophie had been right; the

village was quieter. The High Street was no longer bothered by the boys at the base, complaining about the cigarettes and English coffee, she said. All shipped back to America, taking some of the girls with them and a nursery of screaming mouths, too. It was like before, but with fewer. Those who remained were subdued, skirting the roads like sleepwalkers, heads down. At rare times, a short-ranged barrage of laughter would fly from folk that met with something of the old spirit. But soon as it was picked up it was dropped again, and they carried on in silence. Wounds took time to heal and they weren't sure yet, none of them, quite sure who'd made it back alive.

Sophie ran the household, paying no heed to Ma's way of ordering. Recklessly immune to tradition, she turned everything around so it met her way of thinking. May constantly went looking for things in the wrong place, and in a funny sort of way it made her think of Pa, wondering if that's how he lived in the days of Ma.

To avoid the chaos, she did as asked and spent her time on the allotment, first clearing brambles and speargrass roots that sent her back into the house for gloves. The ground was unwilling to yield at first, turned concrete by the sun's glare. Once it did, May, with sickle in hand, was able to clear a path to the relics of Pa's past planting. She found gooseberry bushes, whose sweet green fruit waited patiently for rescue behind briar thick with thorn, and then plump strawberries, conjuring up an earlier time of him placed near, content and smiling. She made bonfires of the brambles, standing close enough when they burned to get lost in the fog. The earlier stacks smoked powerfully, the remembered smell of Pa's world, bringing with it a prickle of tears that seemed to cleanse past wrongs. She shouldn't stand so close, May thought, gradually releasing herself from its grasp as the work got easier. The Coln kept her company, taking its course down river as it always had. If Sophie could have reversed the flow to send it different, she would have, May thought. While her sister abandoned the old ways, tending Ma inside, May pushed on out. It was slow, tireless work but as weeks went ahead, she sensed progress with the sowing of each new packet of seeds, planting out leeks, cabbages and radishes. She was content to find something of her new self could exist here, too.

They spent their nights, the three of them, curled up on the settee, tuning in to the latest programmes, laughing at radio shows recorded at the BBC. That was in London, May told Honor. They pushed back the furniture and took it in turns to teach her the waltz, which she found old fashioned, Lambeth Walk, ridiculous, and swing, loving, her long limbs advancing through the steps unlike any ten-year-old's. Inside of this fun, May was always aware of Ma above them, silently listening through the boards.

"Just a bit more!" Sophie would shout, flinging herself at the radio to make it scream louder, before flying from them in search of water or, May suspected, something stronger. At those moments, she would turn it down.

"For Grandma," she would say to Honor, putting a finger to her lips.

It was a night like that with Honor asleep on the settee, while May sat in the armchair. The windows were open to the street and a cool breeze waved on in, moving the netting like the summer lived. May looked at Sophie opposite her, draped across the corner of the settee, her leg hooked up over the arm-end. She had just returned from the kitchen and, dosing there, her head bobbed at a careless rate, like moving still to the last played song, a waltz.

"Ain't the old ones the best," she muttered, eyes flickering.

"Sometimes," May said, thinking of the Paramount.

"What happened to your fella?"

"He went missing."

"You lose everything," Sophie accused, chin to her chest, bouncing. It dropped once more and stayed there.

May listened to her turn to sleep, thinking how Sophie had never looked more like Ma than at that moment. She rose quietly and left them both sleeping, closing the door behind. She looked up at the landing, dark and untrodden. In the kitchen, she felt inside the shirt pocket, an old one of Pa's, and found the letter. Still sealed. She opened the back door and stepped out into the night, pulling it closed behind her. Sitting on the step, the stone's coolness was a welcome relief under her. It was good to be outside, leaving the heat with her sister and niece, remembering the dormitory of the Wrenery. May picked up the torch by the step and clicked the switch; blue light lit up the address. Not used to the blackout lift yet, she cupped her hand to make the light small and dim. It sought out the tiny letters that glowed. It wasn't what was wrote there was important, but who had done it. May turned it over and ran her fingers beneath the seal. It puckered unstuck at once to reveal a single sheet.

John McKenzie
29A Selborne Road
Walthamstow
London

2nd July, 1945

Darling May,

It feels odd to put this down on paper and send it with the post. It's like we didn't get done with saying everything face to face and now you're left. I understand, you getting back for your Ma, like you said. I wanted to see Marilyn too. She wouldn't stop kissing me and pulling me tight, like I might go again. Although I told her I wouldn't. You'd be surprised to see me now. She's been feeding me back to health and I do feel something like my old self.

The thing is, darling, you can't know how much I thought of you. During those long nights, and the cold! Well, that chill still finds me, even though it's July and Marilyn says we don't need the fire on. I still do, you know. Think of you often. I've been out some evenings but it isn't the same. I think you're good for me, May, different to the others, and I don't like to go back on a promise. You know what I asked you once and that still stands. Sometimes at night I think of my pals in the lifeboat I couldn't save. They didn't want saving, I think, the ones that went early on. And later, the others didn't have much choice. Don't let's abandon our little ship, May. That sounds damned stupid, I know, coming from a grown man. You write and tell me to come and I will. I'm ready to do that.

Yours, John

May put the light to the bottom of the garden. Beneath the tool shed, a pair of eyes came back. She heard movement in the kitchen behind her and rose, opening the door.

Sophie was at the sink, pouring water into a glass. She looked over, bleary-eyed. May closed the door and drew the curtain across.

"What's that?" Sophie looked at the letter.

"Just a pal in London," May said, stashing it away.

"Oh." Sophie pulled out a chair. "My head!" She groaned, sitting down.

"You got no reason to drink," May said.

"What do you know."

"You got Honor."

"Exactly."

"Is she to blame?"

"I need a drink." Sophie turned in the chair, and started feeling down below the sink.

"Don't," May said going over, already leaning in to pull her away.

Sophie pushed back to get free. "Suppose I asked him to come up to my room?"

"Well, did you?"

"You think that." Sophie had the bottle and was tipping it back like the last ration. She swallowed. "Suppose I invited him to lie there."

"You let him in."

"He had a key." She smiled, the drink coming friendly with her.

"Christopher?"

"You fool!" Sophie's head went back, laughing.

"Who then?" cried May.

They turned; the wireless started up loudly across the hall.

"Now Honor's up," Sophie said, rising, chucking the bottle back beneath the sink.

May followed. Inside the sitting room, Honor was swimming through the air with an imagined partner. The slow steps brought out all sorts of inexperienced sensuality in her face.

"And you can cut that out!" said Sophie, going over and almost severing the knob.

"Oh Ma!" Honor cried. "I love to dance."

"Pa never did," May said, remembering. "Almost made Uncle Richard give it back."

"To who?" said Sophie.

"The Colonel."

It was like that first time in the crypt. Sophie pulled the radio to the floor. It lay in pieces on the carpet along with a couple of shattered tiles from the grate. Honor, backed up against the wall, began to cry. May went to comfort her, wanting really to run and hold the other one, looking across to where Sophie stood now, shaking. The girl didn't understand.

"I'm going to check on Ma," said Sophie, smoothing her dress and going.

May woke early into the chill, her limbs stiff and aching. In the bed beside her, Honor slept peaceful. May freed one arm from beneath the head and rose quietly, putting on her dressing gown and standing in the hall to tie it. In the bathroom, she ran the tap and made contact with a frigid puddle. Next along, the door to Sophie's room stood open, the bed unslept in. It looked exposed and May reached back into the past, remembering earlier times she'd seen it like that. She went down. On the landing below she pushed aside Ma's door. Ma was awake and unmoved, turning her eyes to May when she entered. Beside Ma, sleeping curled in a ball, was Sophie.

In the kitchen, May put the kettle under the tap until the tin splashes were turned to lapping at the rim. She dried her hands and lit the stove. She found bread, arranging it with butter, jam and cups onto a tea tray. Pa's dirty shirt hung still on the back of the chair with the top of the letter sticking out white from the pocket. It was easy to forget there was a question tucked inside, but now May had questions too. How nothing that other thing seemed now compared with this. Had Ma known? Suspected even? The radio Uncle Richard had given was from him; from the Colonel. It wasn't the son after all. It wasn't Christopher. Hadn't the Colonel gone away when Sophie had?

The kettle whistled hot steam. May burnt her hand grabbing up the handle, going in a second time with the cloth. When the pot was ready, she walked it wobbling up the stairs on the tray. Inside the room, light shone on the blankets and its occupants. Ma was propped up by all the pillows with Honor to the left, kept warm beneath her arm. Sophie sat upright, on the other side, brushing at Ma's hair.

After that night of knowing, something calm and unseen let its presence known at the mill cottage. Without fuss, it moved the items in the kitchen cupboards back to their first homes. May had to unlearn every bad habit recently taught by Sophie and reach into the past with fresh-eyed understanding. Some habits, though, were harder to shake than others. She avoided the cupboard beneath the sink until Honor went there once, and glancing over her shoulder, May noticed nothing but the old tin bath, as though it always had the run of it. Ma's room took on a cleanliness not visited upon it for months. Venturing upstairs, May found herself stealing round the corner to try to catch Ma in the act. Watching her frame beneath the covers sharp-eyed in case new shapes appeared, like those made by dusting feathers and broom ends.

It was Sophie who scrubbed the house from attic corner to garden step, stitching and polishing new to purge the life before. For a while, May saw the mill pond run black with all the filth scrubbed up, spilled in. At least the ducks could flap in the gathering suds. Honor was a willing student. Following her ma from morning to night, recording as she went in a small blue book. May thought it clever of her niece. Not calling it up from memory as she had done, but referencing it as fact absolute, noting only one way to wash, and one to scrub.

Not one of them mentioned the wireless again. May took it to the battery and repair shop and sold it for parts. There was enough money to fix the tiles in the grate and buy a pair of dancing shoes for Honor. Even if, for now, she'd have to make do with the songs in her head. The days stretched long and unspoilt like that now, and it was something to sit content in. Content in knowing it wasn't Christopher, but his pa and Uncle Richard tied up one way with knowing all along.

Another week had gone and May made good progress on the allotment now, thinking to next summer even, when life in new colours would shoot skyward to meet a warless world. She was determined that they should grow as before, watching over them as children, as Pa would have done.

Sophie closed the door of the cottage behind and smiled at May across the lane. May stopped digging and waved back, a patch of newly turned earth at her feet. Sophie walked over.

"It's really looking smart, May," Sophie said, coming close, her mouth full scarlet.

"Do you think so?" May stood the spade up tall in the soil.

"Here." Sophie handed her hot tea in a thermos cup. She next unwrapped a cloth. "Brought these, too," and produced sandwiches for lunch.

"But we only live there!" May said.

"Thought we could have them out here," Sophie said. "Honor's watching Ma."

May let herself be guided to the little bench. So often had she watched from the window opposite while Pa sat there, master of the patch he worked harder than all the ones at Big House.

"Coming along nicely, May," Sophie said, handing her a sandwich.

"It's not as good as it was. Do you remember?" May bit into a corner, sharp with pickle.

"Course." Sophie laughed, her eyes turned to the past. "That day when we were children. Do you remember? He had them seeds off that woman knocking door to door."

"He looked like Jack might find the beanstalk!"

"Then Uncle Richard dug them up." Sophie stopped chewing.

"He was always interfering."

"Yes."

"And thick with the Colonel."

"The Colonel?"

"Well, he gave him that radio, didn't he?" May swallowed.

Sophie placed her sandwich down on the paper and licked her lips, keeping her bottom one bitten. There was some seesawing inside her head, May thought, seeing the up and down go there, because it caught her waiting, too.

"I didn't know it was the same one, May, until last night."

"The same as what?"

"One Uncle Richard bragged he'd been given years back. It was a game he liked to play. Showing me how friendly they were; thick as thieves, he said," she turned to May, "with the father of my child."

"But why didn't he tell Pa?"

"It suited him not to."

"But... Pa's brother. He kept it a secret from all of us.

From Ma even?"

Sophie laughed. "It's all such a mess, May. Did I tell you he turned up on account of Honor? After Pa's funeral he came looking for her."

"I saw him in London," she heard herself say.

"We were there. In a flat the Colonel got me. He wanted money then for keeping shut. Seems even the Colonel had had enough of being blackmailed."

"Why didn't you say?" May asked.

"I knew if you saw her regular you'd see it too. Looks like him, don't she?"

They both looked up when a dog barked on the lane, leading someone new towards the village.

"So the Colonel looked after you both?"

"When the fancy took him. He didn't take me on charity, May."

"Oh."

"Don't look at me like that. Didn't I deserve more? It was after carnival that year before I left. Silly old fool supposing I was grateful to win and more besides. Like it's the only thing any of us girls is any good for. Well, I wanted more and I was going to get it, especially after all those years. I heard he was cold to the old lady but I knew how to turn him." Sophie paused and patted the corner of her mouth where she imagined the lipstick had run. "Then when his wife found out, her staring at me like I could just be paid off to go. And I would have been, but for that boy Christopher overhearing and spoiling things. Turning up with all that stolen money when I already had a first class ticket from his pa and a new life away from mine."

"Sophie, no."

"Then Uncle Richard gets wind and wants money from the Colonel to keep quiet, imagining he's found something in it for himself, too. Thinking he's covered his own rotten path good and proper." She smiled like she'd forgotten how to.

"Did Ma know?" May asked quiet.

"Not about the Colonel, but Uncle Richard? Well, she

loved him more than Pa, I reckon, but even then." She sniffed. "Could be I tried to tell her before she got sick."

May put out a hand to her sister's and held it.

"Don't start me off, May. It's done now, all of it." She held up the sandwiches.

May took another. "I saw Christopher on the bridge that day you left."

"Then I'd probably have thought the same," Sophie said, sipping from May's cup. "He probably just wanted to help. She's his sister, you know."

AUGUST

And still John's letter stayed within the top pocket of her shirt. Out on the allotment, it grew dirty, falling to the soil and mixing with the crumbs of earth at her feet. This happened often, so that when May picked it up and blew the dust off, some of it had worked its way beneath the papery fibres, turning them from white to brown like little roots across the page. When it was very hot, it steamed, hanging limply against her breast so that, on bending, she no longer heard it crinkle. At times like these, she reached into the pocket to reassure herself that it remained and hadn't blown into the Coln. Or worse still, floating by, would be picked up by him, his head appearing from the foam to demand an answer there and then. She worried for the words, as though in the summer sweat they'd melt together to form some new, unasked for sentiment. Somehow, having it near, as though she might reply at any hour, helped to convince May it was only inspiration's muse she lacked. She kept a pen in her trouser pocket for its coming on. Ably she believed this waiting, less a crime than not replying at all. Which, remembering with a butterfly-heart each morning that it sat there unanswered still, May had succeeded in so far.

There had been no news of Big House or its occupants. Sophie didn't know or had refused to share more, going back to silence. The chained-up gate remained, barring any sight of what lay beyond. And, as all was still, May suspected Christopher recuperated there, brought back to health and smiles by his loving mother and fiancée. It was enough to think fondly on, what right had she to more? Though it never stopped her turning each time a motorcar took the bridge, as though the memory of him as a boy beside the silver engine in the yard was how he would appear now.

It wasn't his car that beeped blue murder at her from the bridge, but one driven by Rene. May turned to see the red coupé pull up on the gravel outside the sitting room window, raising a hand to her brow to block the sun and frame it there. Even when they clicked the doors shut behind them, Rene went back inside to get at the horn, grinning at May, until she had to run across and stop her.

"Get off, you're muddy!" Rene shooed.

"Serves you right," beamed May.

"Hello darling," said Bridget, greeting her at the trunk-end with a hug that was all chiffon and light.

The cottage door flew open with little care for its hinges and Honor bounded out, alert and bright-eyed. She saw the car and her expression caught between pain and joy. May thought back far to a time when she had been just as taken, going now to put an arm around her niece.

"Rene, this is my sister Sophie's girl, Honor."

"Hello Miss Honor." Rene smiled.

"You're charming," said Bridget, taking Honor lightly by the chin.

She liked the attention and pulled herself up tall and important, mimicking so quickly, as children do, a simpler version of adulthood. Bridget laughed and bent to kiss her cheek.

"Will you come in?" said May.

"I'm telling Ma," said Honor, running ahead.

"It's a little cramped," May said, leading them inside the front room.

"It's charming." Bridget smiled.

May looked, too, thinking how charming could also mean small. "Tea?" she asked, minding her overalls and how they didn't fit the moment, or the one to come.

"May, you didn't say you had friends visiting?" Sophie was one step ahead, appearing in a pale peach tea dress.

"She didn't know," said Rene, standing to shake her hand. "Sorry, we rather just turned up."

"I love surprises," said Sophie, grinning at Bridget and looking at the shawl just rested on the chair end.

Sophie sat opposite them while May went off to make refreshments. Honor was already in the kitchen boiling water, the blue book open on the table.

"Do you mind if I run up and change?" May asked her niece who shook her head and said she better had.

May poked her head around Ma's door and smiled. The woman sat up in bed, a book open on her lap where Sophie had left it. May kissed her on the cheek and turned the page. Up in her room she pulled everything out onto the floor and looked around her naked feet at the pile for something proper. There was an old green and blue checked dress which still fit. She zipped it up and put the collar the right way round in the bathroom mirror. Her nails were filthy. With the little brush she scrubbed away the dirt she could reach and resigned herself to what she couldn't, running barefoot back downstairs to the kitchen.

Honor had a tray ready with cups and spoons arranged side-by-side. They sparkled as though she'd washed them twice.

"What can I do?" May asked.

"Cut that cake," said Honor, pointing at a fat sponge that had appeared upon the table.

May couldn't find the good knife and started off badly with a blunt one, until Honor pulled it from her grip and slid the sharp one across the table.

"Thanks," she mumbled, feeling like Ma had found a way into her niece's head.

They carried everything between them, squeezing in between the laughter of the three in the room.

"What a treat!" said Rene, winking at Honor who returned hers shyly.

Sophie poured while Honor sat on the floor at her feet handing out slices, keeping the broken ones back.

"Your mother tells me you know how to dance?" said Bridget, nibbling on plain sponge.

"Oh, I love to," said Honor, sitting up on her heels, "but we don't have anything to listen to."

"No?" She smiled back. "Then I'll invite you to my next party, so you do."

Honor looked at her mother.

"All of you," offered Bridget.

"Don't tease the girl," said Rene, turning to May. "Thing is, we're on our way to Southampton and came to say goodbye."

"Goodbye?" said May, returning her cup to its saucer.

"We're going to America." Rene and Bridget squeezed hands between them.

"How exciting!" said Sophie.

"We'll stay with Bridget's uncle first in New York, before heading West."

"Are you going to be in a picture?" said Honor, so close to Bridget's face she giggled.

"Yes, I might. Do you think I could?"

"You're beautiful," she replied.

"Oh Rene, congratulations," May said and meant it.

"Now, Miss," said Rene, addressing Honor. "How about a spin?"

Sophie said to go ahead, she'd stay with Ma, while May squashed in after Honor on the tiny backseat.

"Ready?" said Rene, not waiting to see if they were.

She took Mill Lane across the bridge and headed out onto the Cirencester Road.

"The horn, the horn!" cried Honor as they passed a field of sheep who bleated in response.

May rested her head on the leather seat back as they flew past open farmland as lightly as if they were riding on air. In the distance, she saw the corrugated domes of the airbase, empty now, like sleeping giants curled up with their backs towards the sun. They continued on a line with it, until the road pulled away, leaving the giants turned insect as they climbed uphill. The road in front fell from view and it was as though they'd keep climbing, towards the bright blue nothing. They stopped at its summit, looking down upon the village in the distance and all that lay beyond, scattered there like dust shaken from a pan.

May and Rene leant against the hot side of the vehicle whilst Honor led Bridget by the hand across a nearby field.

"How's John?" Rene asked, offering her a cigarette from the pack.

"Fine, I think," she said, taking one and getting it lit on the third attempt.

"You mean you don't know."

"It's not like you and Bridget, Rene," she said, exhaling.

"You were never afraid on your bike."

"It's different." May turned to Rene. "Like it's dressed up as something normal."

"Normal?"

"This marriage business."

"I live to be anything but," said Rene.

Bridget and Honor waved from the top of the stone mound and Rene waved back.

"This anything to do with your old friend?" she said.

May turned away, very sure it had everything.

"You got to be happy, May."

May nodded, feeling them come dampening her hand, pulled beneath an arm that held her, waiting, until she was ready. "Silly, isn't it?" May said, wiping her face.

"Not really," said Rene. Bridget and Honor were returning. "I'm damned scared silly for that one."

Sophie was waiting for them with wrapped sandwiches and cake, for their onward journey, she said, smiling and handing Bridget the parcel, adding, "Oh," before, "you left your scarf."

"Keep it," said Bridget, smiling and getting in again for the off.

"Thanks, May," said Rene, standing close, "for being

such a pal."

"You too. You saved my life that night in Soho."

"And today again, I think," Rene replied, pulling her in tight.

The three stood, waving from the vacated spot while Rene reversed back onto the lane. Bridget's hand went up and the horn sounded twice. Honor followed, running behind, until they turned the corner towards the high street and were gone.

It was a week later that a large sturdy box arrived.

"What's that?" said Sophie, standing aside as two overalled men manoeuvred it in through the sitting room frame.

"Got Honor's name on it," said May, reading the stuck label.

The men drank their tea out front and left. Sophie called Honor and she appeared half-damp still from her wash, hair wet and nightshirt stuck to her shoulders.

"It's for you," they said, pinning the unopened note to her hand and coaxing her forwards.

"For me?" she said, opening it to read. "Oh my goodness!" she said, handing it to Sophie and running towards the box to start work on the lid.

"What a dear sweet girl!" said Sophie, meaning no one present. She handed May the note which, after the formalities, read:

From one dancer to another,

We couldn't take this on the boat and it felt miserable to leave it in the London house. Be a darling and look after it for me, won't you? I've had 78's sent down too, I hope they haven't broken. There are some I do hope you'll like and take the trouble to learn.

Your friend,
Bridget

Honor stood back, wide of eye, while Sophie and May helped lift the rest of the crate away. It stood before them, a deep mahogany sideboard with a roll-top. It took up an entire wall. The top made a pleasing slinking sound as Honor folded it back into the case to reveal a turntable and control board covered in creamy buttons like pearls. May looked at the large grate on front that would shortly emit sound. Ma would feel more than included now.

"Oh, can I play one now?" Honor asked Sophie, clutching a black disc and staring longingly at the needle, as though she might combust at the mere thought of marrying the two.

"If you don't, I will," Sophie said grinning, already winding up the arm to give power.

May left them there, plunging about the sitting room arm-in-arm. Some of the faster tunes she knew as belonging to the night of the party and it made her smile to see Honor enjoying them. May stepped into the back garden and lit a cigarette. An extra, given her by Rene that day in the car, just in case. It didn't taste good like the first, but she smoked it anyway. There was something off, too, about the sky above her head, as though it was riddled with faint, transparent cries. Not of people, but of things. It could have been crashing glass, or wood, or brick, or the crunch of all three. It got tangled in the leafy trees and hedgerows and reverberated down to that small spot, compacted to miniature, so that it wasn't clear what manner or size of object owned it. She thought again of the broken-up greenhouses and drew in a deep suck of smoke which made her cough. May extinguished the cigarette beneath her shoe, hurrying inside to shut the door against further interruptions.

A week passed and what began as the tin-shake rattle of a toolbox of nails grew to such an audible scale, it perverted the bird song and caused the river to run mute. May found they kept the windows closed after it became the thing, barring not just the noise but the assault of a thin plasterlike dust which caught them off guard, turning every surface anaemic, including Ma.

"You said they smashed the greenhouses; they're rebuilding." Sophie said, settling on the obvious.

"I did say that," May said.

It was enough to turn a sane person skipping mad. It was Big House gate, with its heavy lock and chain that stole into her dreams at night. While she slept, she wrestled with it loudly so that she thought it might wake the entire village, changing tact in the lucid early hours, walking imaginary fingers across the iron links to feel out a weakness. None came, and it was always in the waking morning, when the startling curl of sound joined them at the breakfast table, that she thought about striding into the village for the blacksmith with a razor-sharp lie tucked beneath her tongue.

On a morning like that one, fresh with yawns from the night before, May lingered behind Sophie, walking to the high street for provisions while Honor stayed with Ma. It was the sort of lazy morning made you more inclined to drag, than lift feet to walk.

"What you playing at, May?" Sophie said, stopping.

"Nothing," she said, feeling scolded as a child and finding comfort thinking things returned to normal. Shuddering to remember that for Sophie, normal seemed more distant still.

"If you gonna play silly beggars you should have stayed with Honor."

May called up the last image she had of Honor, patience-worn before the gramophone, as though it was to blame and not she for pitting a rising orchestra of noise against the drone outside.

May followed with required lift, past the butcher's window, noting its vast, sanitary air in light of stock. Further by, they passed Pax's, where she saw parts of the radio polished new and offered up like vital parts. Sophie walked on oblivious, swinging empty wicker at her side. May caught up, looking down at the pencilled list in its base as it travelled back and forth.

"Bread, butter and beans," Sophie murmured, and May saw this written there.

They stepped inside the grocers. At the back there was an unknown woman placed behind the confectionery window. She was older than Mrs Layton; pock-marked liked honeycomb, May thought, staring like she'd never been told not to. May thought again of Mrs Layton who'd lost her boys, aligning this loss with the old wrappers and stuck jars. Some of the contents looked like they belonged to Pa's war.

At the front of the shop, Sophie had the list out and was engaged across the counter, laughing like singing, her head thrown back. She had the basket hitched up on the counter, the contents of which heaved over as unnecessarily as she did.

"That wasn't on the list, Sophie," May said, walking front. "Or this." She pulled out a tin of beef not seen for years.

"Careful, Miss." The young man, handsome if you liked that sort of thing, picked up an escaped tomato and placed it back inside the basket.

"It's fine, May," said Sophie, showing her the list. "All done, see?"

Someone had struck out the items and left a series of freshly etched hearts at the foot of the page. The man grinned at her, the stub of a pencil behind his right ear.

"Right then," May said, taking the basket up. "We done here?"

"See you again, Joe," Sophie said, coming behind.

"You didn't have to be rude!" Sophie held the cigarette between her teeth and flicked the match against the open box. "Oh bugger!" she released, sending single sticks flying to meet the road. May bent to collect them.

"I can manage," said Sophie, taking the matches back for the box.

"I know you can," said May rising.

They walked on in silence towards the churchyard,

entering through the gate. Sophie sat down on a stone bench on the path, the unlit cigarette in her hand. May fitted beside her, the basket on the floor at her feet.

"You've done a good job, you know, with Honor," May said, taking the box in hand and striking the match. She held it cupped there, inviting Sophie and the cigarette.

"I know," Sophie said, moving towards it.

A drag of parishioners went past, nodding at them, before going in for service. Sophie hid the cigarette at the back of the bench and the two giggled.

"How long you planning on staying?" May said, holding her breath and hand out for a smoke.

"This is my home, isn't it?"

"And what if he comes back?" May asked, blowing.

"He wouldn't dare." Sophie lit fresh. "Besides, there's Ma to think of."

"That's good, Sophie, really good." May looked towards the church, recognising the face looking back. "Shall we go in?"

"Better get back for Ma," said Sophie. "You go ahead," she said, looking at the woman who stood now for both to see. Sophie smiled across and, with the basket, headed back past the stones.

"Hello dear," the woman said.

"Hello," said May, going over.

She hadn't changed. Clipped like a church display, but frail as the glass vessel that held it.

"I haven't seen you, May, well, since that night." Reverend Hunniford's widow spoke thin, like paper. She was altered after all. Not in appearance, but speech. Doubt in the ever after, had found its way in through her loss.

"You're back, though?" May tried, her tone reduced to match.

"No, dear, only as the warden. I look after the flowers now." She looked at her hands, as though expecting to find pruning shears or the stem of some perennial. "Will you come and see them?"

"I think I will," said May, smiling and stepping inside.

The new vicar led them in prayers of remembrance, redemption and rebirth. May thought of Sophie's shopping list. Getting the items stuck in her head, recanting them faithfully as those around spoke the Lord's Prayer. Life wasn't ordered to plan. The basket filled to the brim with new and unexpected things. She looked up. The brilliant windows had survived intact. Above the altar, the light through the central scene transformed the thin congregation into something fruitful and alive. They were transfixed, sitting humble against pew backs, praying gratitude on high that they'd come through. The front benches sat empty and May yearned seeing them so, turning restless each time a light summer blow caught the main door in its creak. The Reverend Hunniford's widow rose to fasten it and smiled at May, returning to her seat at the back.

Sophie was staying. May could pray for that. Give thanks for the peace that mended away at her sister's heart, working still at the fracture there. The future had about it the promise of happiness, for each of them if they wanted it. Why then, did it not extend to John? Thudding ungratefully against her chest, she blamed her own spoilt heart while acknowledging, in His house who saw everything, that the fault was hers.

The congregation rose. She hadn't noticed it was over. May joined, filing through the shade to emerge, squinting into the sun, caught amidst the tight huddle of parishioners who loitered, departing thanks on the vicar. She failed to find Mrs Hunniford again and was circled about by bits of conversation instead.

"It's caused a calamitous mess," said the wife.

"We'll finally get some sleep," replied the husband.

"Them's not comin' back."

"I can well believe it, Joan."

"Who's not coming back?" May said.

"Colonel and Lady Barker, Miss." The wife pushed front.

"Have they sold Park House?"

"No, Miss," laughed the husband. "Pulled the whole lot down, brick by brick."

May lasted out another week, stumbling between the kitchen and the sitting room, picking up things, moving them, helping with the washing, the scrubbing and anything that needed doing, or didn't.

"You sure there's nothing wrong?" Sophie asked.

"Yeah Aunt May," Honor put in, their heads in a collective rise to eye her suspiciously.

"I'm fine," came her response. Even Ma, when May bent beneath the bed to sweep the dust away, found a way to let her know she suspected something was wrong, tilting her head in a previously unseen fashion.

So it was Big House that lay like a shroud upon their lives. For weeks it crept beneath the door frames and in at the windows, its dust never getting clean away. Some of it was pink-hued, like the paint upon the walls of the drawing room she remembered, or brick-red, like at Stable Court. The different colours stained the cleaning water when she poured it away, leaving the residue of plastered silt in the bottom of the bucket like it could be worked up and used fresh. May was driven to sleepless nights by the new silence, more so than when the destruction could be heard. But, she hadn't known what it was then and there was a certain thrill in the unexpected churn of it. Almost like when waiting for the carnival floats to emerge, forged in secret within locked sheds. Now, the silence pressed heavy against her chest and when she crept late at night to her bedroom window to seek out any clue across the fields, her heart sank at realising all that remained was hidden from view behind the trees.

It was when out working one afternoon that May hit upon the idea. Freeing the sharpened shovel from the soil, she closed the allotment gate behind her and crossed the bridge, arriving in front of Big House gate. May picked up the brittle chain to feel the weight of it. It was heavier than in her dreams and the rust stained her hands. She lifted the spade, sliding the sharp end into the space between the door and the links, sealing tension there. She looked around before throwing her whole weight behind the handle. The force sprung back at her along with the shovel. Thrown, she sat up on the path with the tool at her side whilst the chain swung pendulum, intact. May rose, picking up the shovel again and taking the chain in her other hand, saw where a rusted link had freed itself from the teeth. She raised the blade again and fixed it firmly in the gap, leaning surely on the handle to increase the pressure, and with a deafening whack, assaulted it again. This time, she only flew back a little. It was the chain that sprung away, snaking to the floor at her feet. The shovel blade looked gnarled. She rested it against the wall and kicked the chain to one side, reaching out with both hands to raise the latch and step inside.

What had she expected to find? In the destructive wilderness of change, that for years had run them all aground, not so much as a leaf had slipped here. She sighed, releasing a cry into the unmoved beauty of it all. The Serpentine meandered slippery and cool through the land as before, enveloped on both sides by nature's crawl. A team of birds drifted carefree across the surface and she imagined them blinking welcome at her finally come, asking what had kept her away, as though war's long charge was nothing to them nor time neither. May wiped her dirty hands on her trousers, feeling like a stranger to this place. She walked along the bank, coming level with the boathouse on the opposite side, surprised to see it standing still. A small forgotten rowing boat bobbed against its berth inside.

She sat on the springy grass beneath the leaves of a sycamore and stretched her legs in front. Wanting to touch the blades bare-toed, May drew her boots up and unlaced, tugging the socks off afterwards. Laying down in the grass, she felt the sun strike out between the leaves, catching her in its heat. A while later, a duck splashed noisily and she sat up on her elbows to watch it beat cool water from its wings. It felt a crime to lie there, turning in the heat, growing lazy beneath its rays. Especially now she was here. She stood, glancing further up the bank towards where the stone bridge sat and then back the way she'd come; she was the only one. May reached a hand to her trouser buttons and moved

quickly, wriggling the material to her ankles. She lifted the
shirt above her head and added it to the pile, standing still in
her underwear, enjoying the feel of cool air over liberated
skin. But still, it didn't come close. Not to the memory of
freer times. The elastic around her waist and back caught up
her skin, red-marked and rashed by prickly heat. She
unhooked herself and slid outside, becoming skin. May
walked towards the bank and raising her hands above her
head, dived in.

It was deeper than the mill pond. She continued her
descent, thinking it might go on forever calling her
downwards, until turning, she ascended for air, rationing her
reserves for another drop below the velvet surface. May
lapped in spirals beneath the sheen, feeling the tug of water
rush against all of her. She stretched her limbs into the green
abyss, catching up weed and plant life between her fingers.
When she next surfaced, she couldn't remember what it was
to be on land, seeing her clothing on the bank as things
belonging to another. The shirt not Pa's, nor the grey
trousers folded neatly on top of a pair of shoes, which, in
reality were far too big. She heard a splash and turned to see
Christopher swimming towards her.

He smiled, staying on the periphery of where the water
moved in circles around her. She dipped her head below to
rise again, seeing him there still, close enough to touch. He
uttered the beginnings of a word, but was silenced by a
spray of water pushed across the surface. He spluttered,
splashing back in return, before they slipped together
beneath the surface to continue at play below. His limbs
were naked just like hers, invisible in the gloom, each
knowing that submerged they were the same being. May
wrestled playfully from his grasp as he did hers and coming
up for air, discovered herself held, as she held him. They
broke apart and breathless, swam towards the bank, falling
upon the grass to start again.

It was different to before, when they'd seemed like

children. When she'd not seen the truth of it. That untruth had its heyday in a different time and place. She had been witness to pain and death, seeing friends and loved ones knocked into oblivion, as he had, but with its passing, came newfound tenderness and understanding. This is what they'd come to experience. It made her wonder to remember it again as they helped each other on with their clothes, glancing at the patch of grass as though it were the only proof they'd cared so completely.

Dressed, they laughed and walked together towards the stone bridge. The afternoon, turning to night, spread shadows at their feet.

"I know what you did for Sophie, you did to help," May said.

"No." He stopped, freeing her hand from his grip. "I wanted her to leave, so Father would stop hurting mother."

"It was right to want that," she said.

They walked onwards, reaching the bridge. She looked past his shoulder to the empty space where the house should have been, abandoned to endless rivets of ploughed farmland. Christopher held her hand tight, leading her across and through the soil, pointing to where an office had been, his mother's desk looking out on the garden, and to where the car had stood before it was sold. They ended at a vast series of concrete slabs which had been the greenhouse complex.

"But why?" May asked

"We had to," he replied. "The army made such a mess of things."

"Look." She let go and went over to a small crop of marrows and pumpkins. There was order in their placement.

"He was a kind man," he said, joining her. "And a decent gardener. Father said so."

They walked back towards the bridge, stopping in the middle. Christopher leant against the side and looked out at the water.

"It's good it's gone," he said, "and so have Mother and

Father."

"Where?" she asked, going to his side.

"France, to start again."

"And you?"

"Some deeds to the land to sign over, and other things." His face became serious. "When I saw you in London…" he said, looking towards the mill.

"Yes."

"You said you were engaged."

"I did, didn't I?"

"I'm going away, you see."

"To France?"

"Never there," he said, turning to look at her. "Where would you go, May?"

"Ask Georgie, not me," she teased.

"She ran off with an American from the base, or rather, I encouraged her to." Christopher looked down into the water and stifled a laugh. "A rough and tumble sort of chap."

She thought of Wanda. Perhaps she'd write with John's address.

"That's funny," she said.

"It is, isn't it?" He smiled back.

Christopher looked beyond her to where the house once lay. At the end of the field the sun slipped off the horizon before reaching high once more. It was remarkable. He watched the last of the light dance across the land before it rested on May, catching at her golden crown.

Fantastic Books
Great Authors

CROOKED
CAT

Meet our authors and discover
our exciting range:

- Gripping Thrillers
- Cosy Mysteries
- Romantic Chick-Lit
- Fascinating Historicals
- Exciting Fantasy
- Young Adult and Children's
  Adventures

Visit us at:
www.crookedcatbooks.com

Join us on facebook:
www.facebook.com/crookedcatbooks

Printed in Great Britain
by Amazon